THE
HANDSOME PRINCE

THE

HANDSOME PRINCE

GAY EROTIC ROMANCE

EDITED BY
NEIL PLAKCY

CLEIS
PRESS

Published in the United States by Cleis Press, Inc., 2246 Sixth Street, Berkeley, California 94710.

Printed in the United States.
Cover design: Scott Idleman/Blink
Cover photograph: Elie Bernager/Getty Images
Text design: Frank Wiedemann
Cleis Press logo art: Juana Alicia

ISBN-13: 978-1-57344-659-4

Contents

INTRODUCTION

We all know the fairy tale. The handsome prince comes riding up on his white stallion and with a single kiss rescues the beautiful princess from her enchantment. Then they ride off together to live happily ever after.

But what if the person longing for that handsome prince is a man? I love the way the stories in this anthology find so many ways of turning the story into something very different, but with the same outcome.

This book is a mix of traditional and contemporary stories, each with its own unique fairytale atmosphere. Sometimes the prince is the one who needs rescuing, as in "Chauffeur Prince" and "Creosote Flats and the Big Spread." Sometimes the true prince is the other guy, like in "The Virgin Prince and the Rebel Chief" and "Reckless." There is humor and charm in these stories, with an underlay of passion and desire.

The one thing these stories have in common, along with the original fairy tales, is a happy ending. Whether it's a HEA—

happily ever after—or a HFN—happy for now—when these guys find their princes, hot steamy sex ensues.

Here's to stories (and heroes) that make us swoon!

Neil Plakcy

THE MASTER

Fox Lee

At twenty-one, Xiao's bachelorhood had officially become peculiar. The only son and eldest child of the Xie family, he had refused every attempt his parents made to arrange a marriage for him. The people in the village called Xiao too picky. If he didn't lower his standards, they said, he would never get married. Xiao was not bothered by such speculation. What kept him up at night was the idea that someone in the village might begin to suspect his true self.

Xiao had known for years that he had no feelings for women. When he was young, he assumed that he simply lacked romantic passion. As got older, however, he realized the problem was not in his heart, much less his libido. He was relieved, then, when his parents threw up their hands, declared him too stubborn for his own good, and turned their attentions to his sister, Wei.

Wei was a beautiful young woman, with many admirers in the village. Xiao was sure she would marry quickly and, with any luck, produce enough grandchildren to thoroughly distract his parents. His mother and father were in less of a rush to marry their daughter off. They wanted to be sensible about the matter and consider each potential son-in-law carefully.

They waited too long. Wei was still single when an official from the city arrived in search of a third wife. The official's name was Ai-Fu, and he walked with the air of an expected, and honored, guest. The entire village knew he was trouble. As soon as he saw her, Ai-Fu announced that Wei would be his.

Xiao's father drank heavily that night and could be heard across the village cursing the heavens for his family's misfortune. It was well known that Ai-Fu was not a kind or patient man. His riches meant nothing; once Wei became a married woman, it would be as if she had never been a part of her previous family. Xiao's parents would never see her again, much less have a chance to cherish their grandchildren.

The next morning, Wei was gone. She left behind a short note pinned to a blanket.

I am sorry, but I will not marry such a man. My heart belongs to another.

The son of their neighbor was also missing. It did not take much imagination to realize that the two had run off together. Ai-Fu would be back in half a month, and he would not forgive such a profound loss of face.

The village elders came that evening to consult with the Xie family. Many suggestions were offered, including faking Wei's death; however each carried too much risk. The elders concluded that there could be but one reasonable outcome: The Xie family would have to face Ai-Fu and beg his mercy. Xiao's parents silently agreed that there was no choice. Xiao refused to be so accommodating.

"This is your plan?" He demanded of the elders. "That my family sacrifice itself to the whim of Ai-Fu?"

"Forgive my son," Xiao's father quickly interjected. "I'm

afraid these recent events have made him emotional."

"How else should I be?" Xiao asked. "Do you think Ai-Fu will accept your apology and go on his way? The three of us will die, for the sake of his ego!"

"There is no way around it," his father said. "We cannot ask the village to stand up for us. Ai-Fu will come with a caravan to escort his bride home. His men will turn on anyone who defies him."

Xiao's father placed his hand on his son's shoulder. Xiao turned away, and his eyes flashed outrage.

"I will not let you suffer for your sister. You will leave, and go to the North."

"I will stand by my parents. If it is to the death, then so be it," Xiao spat.

Elder Han stepped forward. Though the oldest of the elders by far, he had been in the village scarcely more than ten years. No one knew much about him, except that he was a widower whose wife had died in childbirth.

"Perhaps," Elder Han said gently, "there is another way. What you require is a hero, one whose heart could be turned by your plight."

"A hero?" Xiao scoffed. "And where would we find one?"

"In the woods," Elder Han said. "Three days walk from here. Five if you get lost."

Silence fell on the group. Xiao became indignant. If there was someone who could help his family, he wanted to know who it was and how to find him.

"Well?" he asked. "Have you all lost your tongues?"

His mother and father gasped, but Elder Han chuckled. The other elders did not.

"You mean Kai-Rong," one of them said grimly. "Only one part of that man can be moved, and it is not his heart."

"Do you always listen to rumors?" Elder Han asked. "And if he is what people say, would his swords be any less sharp?"

"Tell me who this person is," Xiao said. "I will find him, and give him whatever he wants in return for his protection."

All the elders, save for Elder Han, shook their heads. "Who is Kai-Rong?" Xiao's mother asked. "Is he a dangerous man?"

"To his enemies," Elder Han replied, "and I doubt he has many left. Kai-Rong lives in the forest around the mountain, and keeps his own company."

"Would he help us?" Xie asked. "And if he will, what will he want in return? I will remind you, Elder Han, that I have already lost a daughter."

Xiao was tired of so much talking with no action. The curious looks from the elders and the tense expression on his father's face increased his impatience. Xiao looked between his father and Elder Han, willing them to speak plainly to him.

"*Aiyaa*," Elder Han exhaled loudly. "There are bigger concerns than who a man takes to his bed. Your son is old enough to know that there are men who sleep beside other men."

Xiao's mother's eyes went wide.

"You want to use my son to seduce this person? I will not allow it!"

"Calm yourself," Xiao's father told her. "Our son will go to the North. We will not hang our hopes on some elusive master who preys on young men."

"I will leave tomorrow," Xiao said.

"Did I speak too softly?" His father asked. "You will stay here, until we can arrange your trip to the North."

"I will find Kai-Rong and convince him to defend us against Ai-Fu."

Xiao's father shook with anger. Their words grew heated, until Elder Han was forced to step between the two.

"Enough! Your son will use his mind and words to sway Kai-Rong, not his body. And if Xiao cannot convince him, then you are no worse off than you already are. He will come home, and be sent to the North."

Xiao's father stared at Elder Han. When he spoke, his words were cold.

"Very well, Elder Han. But as you put this plan in my son's head, let his fate be in your hands."

Xiao's father spent another night drowning his frustrations in wine, while Xiao's mother pleaded with him to reconsider his rash decision. Xiao was immovable. He got little sleep, yet felt alert and energized when Elder Han showed up the next morning. Xiao was grateful for the company, even if Elder Han was taking him only as far as the forest's edge. Xiao took the opportunity to ask about Kai-Rong.

"What kind of weapons does he use?"

"Butterfly swords," Elder Han told him. "People say he could fight off an army with them."

"Then why does he live alone?"

"It is troublesome for a master to live among others: Someone always wants to start a fight. Also, a man like Kai-Rong can never know whom to trust. People will lie to a master's face, and betray him in the worst ways, to get him to do their dirty work."

"It sounds like a tortured life," Xiao said.

He had another question, one he didn't dare ask. Xiao wanted to know if men like Kai-Rong ever found someone to love them. He shook off the melancholy thought as he and Elder Han reached the edge of the forest.

"You are a good boy," Elder Han told him. "Stubborn, like my own son. He was born when I was already an old man, you know. The only reason I have lived this long is to worry about him."

Elder Han reached into his garments and took out a package wrapped in cloth. "Ah, but that's an old story. Take these sweets. They'll help you get on Kai-Rong's good side."

Xiao thanked the elder and bowed deeply before continuing on his way. The air was cooler among the trees, and the silence almost deafening. Xiao stood still, until the normal sounds of the forest resumed. He chided himself for getting spooked; it wasn't as if he had never been in the woods before. Yet on those occasions he had company with him, and their course was clear. Kai-Rong's whereabouts were vague. Xiao knew which direction to walk in, but not much else. He told himself it was enough. If good fortune was on his side, he would find Kai-Rong.

Days passed with no sign of the martial arts master, nor any other human being. By the fourth day, Xiao worried that time was running out. He was relieved when he suddenly heard rustling nearby, too loud to be anything but a large body moving through the underbrush. It might not be Kai-Rong, Xiao cautioned himself, but whoever it was might know where to find him.

Small trees and bushes parted, as a tiger strolled into the clearing. It stopped to look Xiao over, as if unsure whether the human was worth the trouble of killing. Xiao took no chances. He dropped his pack, ran for the nearest tree, and scaled it like a crazed monkey. When he looked down from his perch, he saw that the tiger had gone after more convenient prey, the food in Xiao's pack. Anything the tiger had no use for was torn and strewn about the small clearing. By the time the big cat went away, Xiao had nothing but the clothes on his back and a small knife attached to his belt.

With his supplies destroyed, Xiao was in a foul mood the rest of the day. Lost in his own self-pity, he didn't pay attention to where he was going or to the forest around him. He nearly walked into low-hanging branches, and at one point traveled in a circle that brought him back to the clearing. When night came, it didn't take long for him to stumble over his own feet. Xiao fell with a heavy thump that drove the air out of his lungs. There was a dull rustle, and hot pain stabbed him between his neck and shoulder. Xiao rolled away in time to see the long, dark body of a snake slither into the darkness.

He had no way to tell what kind of snake it was, only that, if it was poisonous, he was in great danger. Though Xiao had a knife to open the wound, there was no way to see where the bite was, nor reach it with his mouth. His fears were confirmed as his mind clouded over and his vision faded. Darkness threatened to swallow Xiao completely; then a pair of hands shook him.

"Can you hear me?" a man's voice asked. "Can you speak?"

Xiao dug into what little strength he had and managed to say the word, "Snake."

"Where?" the voice asked.

The words wouldn't come. Xiao let his head fall to the side to expose the wound.

"Hold still," the man told him. "This will hurt."

Cold metal kissed Xiao's flesh and sliced across his neck. He felt blood trickle down his chest, then warm, wet pressure as the man applied his mouth to the cut. Every few seconds he stopped, to spit out the mixture of venom and Xiao's blood. Xiao groaned, and a hand touched the side of his face. It was cool against his skin: a welcome respite from the fire that seemed to rage from the very core of him.

"It will be all right," the man said. "I'll take care of you."

More of the toxin was sucked out of Xiao's neck, yet his symptoms spread. Every part of him ached, while his body temperature switched without warning between hot and cold. The stranger told him not to be afraid, as he cradled Xiao in his arms and lifted him up.

* * *

"How do you feel?"

It was the same voice that Xiao heard in the forest. He opened his eyes and blinked against the light, surprised to no longer be outside.

"Ah, you heard me this time! Good boy."

Fingertips brushed hair away from Xiao's forehead. They lingered, stroking the skin lightly. Xiao saw that he was lying on a floor mat, with a blanket over him. To his left, a man knelt on the floor. He was older than Xiao by five years or more. The man's robe was open to the waist: Xiao glimpsed a smooth, defined chest, with lightly tanned skin. Dark hair fell freely across the man's back and shoulders as he helped Xiao into the seated position.

"Do you remember what happened?" the man asked.

"A snake bit me," Xiao said. "I must have frightened it when I fell."

"You were lucky I was looking for you," the man said. "I found your things a few miles away, next to a set of tiger pawprints. I worried that someone might be hurt, so I tracked you. My name is Cheng."

"I am Xiao."

Xiao pressed a hand against his head. There was a deep pain behind his eyes, pounding against his skull.

"Your head will hurt for a few days while your body heals. You can stay here until your strength returns."

"I can't stay," Xiao said, "I have to find someone, a man named Kai-Rong."

The man's brow furrowed. "Kai-Rong left years ago, for the North. It would take months to find him, if he even let you."

Xiao's blood ran cold. If Kai-Rong was in the North, then there was no hope for Xiao's mother and father.

"What did you need to see him about?" Cheng asked.

"My family requires his protection. An official from the city is going to kill them. He chose my sister as his third wife, but she ran away, and left my parents to answer for her."

"I am sorry to hear that," Cheng said. "Sadly, I have nothing to offer but my hospitality."

"I have another week to search," Xiao said. "Do you know of anyone else who could help me?"

"Xiao," Cheng said, "you have been ill for three days. It will take you another day, at least, before you can walk."

The words shattered against Xiao's ear. At best, he could get back to the village in time to die with his parents.

Cheng tried to make conversation as he tended to Xiao over the course of the day. He told Xiao not to lose heart. The official could be lenient, and forgive. Xiao pretended to consider Cheng's words. That night, when he was sure the other man was asleep, Xiao prepared to leave. All he had to do was concentrate, he told himself, and he could walk. Then fate might take pity on him and reveal a way to save his parents.

Xiao made it outside, and a few steps further, before his legs turned to water and he crashed to the ground. Cheng awoke and hurried to his side.

"What are you doing?" he asked.

"I'm not going to sit here like an invalid! I'll get home, if I have to crawl on my hands and knees."

Xiao was angry at himself for not finding Kai-Rong; at his sister, for betraying the family; and most of all at Ai-Fu, a cocky rich man who thought he could take whatever he wanted.

"Don't you understand?" Cheng asked. "There is no choice in the matter. The toxin from the snake damaged your body. You're lucky to be alive."

Xiao laughed. "I'm going to die anyway. At least I had hope, before I talked to you." A fresh wave of despair hit him as he spoke.

Cheng, meanwhile, looked to be deep in thought. "Something has occurred to me," he told Xiao. "No one else knows Kai-Rong left for the North. I could go in his place."

"To what end?" Xiao asked. "You're too young to pass for him."

"You think a master has to be an old man, with white hair?" Cheng asked. "Kai-Rong built his reputation as a teenager, when he was wild and undisciplined. Once he got older, he saw that it was foolish to fight for the sake of fighting and moved out here."

"Can you fight?"

"With Kai-Rong's reputation, I won't have to. Ai-Fu won't want to lose any more face than he already has."

Xiao wasn't convinced. Kai-Rong's reputation might not have reached the city at all. The elders had kept it from an entire generation in the village, despite living in the shadow of the mountain Kai-Rong once called home.

"It's worth a try, don't you think?" Cheng asked.

"If Ai-Fu calls your bluff, he will kill you too."

"I am an optimistic man," Cheng said. "And I knew Kai-Rong well. I can be his mimic. If I bring my father's old sword, I'll look like a real warrior."

"Kai-Rong uses butterfly swords."

"Some people keep the two butterfly swords sheathed as one. Who can tell unless I take it out? Besides, Ai-Fu will be too afraid to think much about it."

It was a fool's plan. Perhaps, Xiao thought, it would also have a fool's luck.

"You may be too optimistic," he told Cheng. "But I thank you, for myself, and for my family."

"Don't be so serious," Cheng scolded him. "You'll give me nightmares."

Back inside his home, Cheng laid beside Xiao on the bed and slipped his arm around the younger man's waist.

"This is so you can't sneak away," he said.

It wasn't long before Cheng was sound asleep. Xiao remained wide awake. He had never shared a bed so intimately with a man before. Xiao could feel Cheng's body heat through the thin linen robes both men wore. It struck him that Cheng spoke of Kai-Rong as if the two had either been best friends or, as Xiao suspected, lovers. He turned onto his other side so that he could face Cheng. The older man continued to sleep, unaware of the attention. Cheng's lips were parted slightly, an unintended invitation.

It was only fair, Xiao told himself. One furtive kiss, to make up for all the ones he would never get to have. Cheng's arm loosened around the younger man's waist, as Xiao lightly pressed their lips together. Xiao's body flushed, and his heart throbbed. He was going to pull away, when the arm across his back slid up, and a hand cupped the back of his head. Cheng's lips parted further, and his tongue urged Xiao's to do the same. Xiao complied, and felt himself grow hard as they explored each other's mouths.

Their hands tugged at each other's clothing, pulling the fabric away to expose the skin underneath. Xiao whimpered, overwhelmed, as Cheng moved on top of him and nibbled his way down Xiao's chest. Cheng's mouth licked and sucked the left nipple, while his fingers made lazy circles around the right, then trailed away to reappear around Xiao's shaft. Cheng's mouth abandoned Xiao's chest and hovered near his ear.

"Have you done this before?" Cheng asked.

"No."

"Don't worry. I will be careful."

At his family's home, there was rarely any privacy. Xiao had few opportunities to touch himself, and it was always done as quickly as possible. Xiao was embarrassed at how little time it took before he spilled his seed into the other man's mouth. Cheng stayed at the end of the floor mat, and Xiao felt something cold and wet touch his anus. Cheng's finger swirled and probed against it, until the ring of muscles yielded.

"Do you like this?" Cheng asked.

"Yes. No one has ever touched me there."

Cheng added another finger and continued to stroke Xiao from the inside. His erection was back, as hard as before. Cheng leaned forward to kiss Xiao's chest and stomach.

Cheng withdrew his fingers and replaced them with the tip of his cock. He entered slowly so that Xiao could stretch around him. Xiao moaned, too weak to do anything but accept the pleasure, as Cheng picked up speed. Xiao came again, and in the next breath felt Cheng pulse inside of him.

"It's been a long time," Cheng murmured, when it was over.

His hands caressed Xiao's thighs, as if trying to memorize the feel of his skin.

"Longer for me," Xiao told him.

Cheng drew him close, and locked Xiao in a kiss.

"If I had my way," he said, "neither of us would ever have to wait again."

By the time Xiao regained his strength, there were only two and a half days left to reach the village. Cheng said it was more than enough time since he knew the woods so well. At Xiao's insistence, they walked both day and night. The only exceptions were short breaks for Cheng to massage Xiao's legs. If not for his skilled hands, Xiao knew he would have crippled himself in his fervor to get home.

They arrived at the village in the early afternoon. Xiao's parents had already been bound with ropes and dragged from their home by Ai-Fu's men. Xiao wanted to run to them, but Cheng held him back.

"Forgive me," Cheng said softly. "My heart believed you, but I needed to see it with my eyes."

He approached Ai-Fu without a trace of fear. Ai-Fu looked down from his horse and sneered at Cheng.

"Who is this stray dog?" he called out.

"My name is Kai-Rong. What business do you have in this village?"

"You dare ask about my business?" Ai-Fu grinned maliciously. "I came to collect my bride, yet I find she has been allowed to elope with some worthless human filth."

"No doubt," Cheng said, "she preferred him to the alternative."

Two of Ai-Fu's men came forward, hands on the hilts of their long swords. The remaining six watched Ai-Fu, awaiting instruction.

"I should not be surprised," Cheng said. "A man who picks on the elderly cannot be expected to participate in his own battles. How many of them do I have to kill to win the Xie family's freedom?"

Ai-Fu sat back in the saddle and stroked his chin in mock contemplation.

"There are four people: an old man and woman, an ungrateful girl, and an idiot son. I believe that is worth all eight of my men."

Elder Han stepped out of the crowd of villagers, his expression beatific. "May I say one thing, to commemorate this occasion?"

"Why not?" Ai-Fu replied. "It's not every day I get to see so many fools die."

"Thank you," Elder Han said. "I would like to say that, like the Xie family, I have only one son. He is the reason my hair is white, and my skin is more wrinkled than a turtle's. For years, I worry about him. Now I do not need to worry any more. Thank you, Ai-Fu, for bringing this happy day. It is too bad you will be dead soon."

Elder Han ended the brief, bewildering statement, and folded his hands contentedly in front of him.

The man Xiao knew as Cheng turned to Xiao and smiled. "You see why I don't visit him? He loves to hear himself talk. When I was a child, I used to pray to go deaf."

Kai-Rong turned back to Ai-Fu, and reached for his sheath. A second later he stood ready to fight, a gleaming butterfly sword in each hand.

AUGUSTUS WOODS AND THE PRINCE OF ROCK 'N' ROLL

Aaron Michaels

A ugustus Woods thought love was a bunch of hooey. Something for the namby-pamby types to gush about when they had a partner or to cry in their beers about when they didn't. Who in his right mind needed a thing like that?

Lust, now—Gus was a big fan of lust. As far as Gus was concerned, lust was the best damn thing in the world. Hard bodies and harder cocks, maybe a kiss or two to get the old engine revving, then get right down to business. Gus was good with getting down to business.

"You're gonna die alone," Gus's friend Lola always told him when they were out drinking at Diamond Pete's, their favorite watering hole. "A shriveled up old queen whose dick don't work no more. Who'd want that?"

Lola, who'd started off life as Lonnie, had kissed her own dick good-bye years ago, so Gus thought she was a fine one to talk. Lola was always falling in and out of love, but Gus was pretty sure the sincerity level of Lola's brand of love was about equal to the sentiment inside a 99¢ Wal-Mart valentine plucked from the bargain bin on February 15.

Then Gus met Louis, and everything changed.

Louis—pronounced Lou-*ee!*—Dupont. Lead singer and front man for Cracked Visions, a small-time band with big-time aspirations.

Gus, never a music connoisseur, wasn't sure what kind of music Cracked Visions played. He wouldn't have given the band a second thought beyond wondering what the hell Pete had been thinking when he let a noisy bunch of wannabe rock stars pollute the fine atmosphere of Diamond Pete's, but then Gus caught sight of the lean, tousle-curled lead singer strutting on the little behind-the-bar stage like he owned the place.

Dressed in tight, black leather pants that left nothing to the imagination and a white silk shirt open to his navel, the singer had the complete attention of every straight woman and gay man in the bar the minute he set his dusty-booted foot on stage. His chin sported a minimal amount of stubble, and his dark hair came almost to his shoulders. His singing voice, when he wasn't screaming out lyrics, was surprisingly deep and melodic. His brown eyes smoldered beneath lids outlined in black and smudged with gray shadow.

When those eyes lighted on Gus seated at his regular stool, second to the last on the left side of the bar, Gus felt a rush of electricity zing straight through him to his cock. That, Gus was familiar with—good old lust come a-calling. If he hadn't felt that rush of lust in the vicinity of someone as edible as the sinful singer gyrating less than a dozen feet in front of his face, Gus might have wondered if his cock had shriveled up and died on him when he wasn't looking.

What did take Gus by surprise was the giant-sized fist that grabbed hold of his heart and squeezed for all it was worth.

"Shut your mouth, you're gonna catch flies." Lola had to yell in his ear through the sheer volume of noise coming off the stage, and even then, Gus barely heard her.

"Huh?" Gus asked, though he didn't really care. He couldn't peel his eyes away from the lead singer, who was doing moves in those tight leather pants that would put Elvis to shame.

Lola chuckled. "You got it bad. And can I say, it's about time."

Lola was making less sense than usual. Gus let her laugh. He was having trouble breathing, his chest still felt tight, and if he hadn't felt so damn good in a shaky kind of way he might have thought he was having a heart attack.

In fact, Gus felt so good he sat through the band's entire act. He forgot about Lola. He even forgot about finishing his beer. All he could think about was getting the singer with the sinful body and shadowed eyes into a dark corner somewhere and fucking the living hell out of him.

Except the mere thought of meeting the man made Gus nervous. What was up with that? Gus never got nervous, not about random hookups. And he never, ever went for guys who wore makeup.

What the hell was wrong with him?

By the time the last chord bounced off the walls, the bar was mostly empty, and Gus chalked the whole thing up to a bad bunch of beer nuts. Better to go home and forget about the whole thing.

He was about ready to do just that when Lola waved at the band. Lola stood six foot four and still had linebacker shoulders holding up the spaghetti straps of her top. When Lola waved, everyone paid attention.

"Excuse me," Lola said. "My friend here would like to buy you all a drink."

The rest of the band—two guitarists, a bass player, and a drummer—stopped putting their instruments away and looked at Lola. The lead singer's eyes slid from Lola to Gus. "This your friend?" he asked in a husky, raw-sounding voice.

Gus felt his cheeks heat up. What the fuck? He *never* blushed.

"That's him," Lola said. "He wants to tell you how much he enjoyed your music."

Lola's dark eyes danced with gleeful good humor. If Gus wasn't sure Lola could still beat him senseless if she had a good mind to, he'd clamp a hand over her mouth to hush her up and quick-step her right on out the front door of Diamond Pete's.

The corners of the singer's mouth turned up just the slightest. "I never turn down a free drink."

"Isn't that just wonderful!" Lola said.

Yeah, wonderful. Good thing Diamond Pete—who, as far as Gus knew, didn't have a diamond to his name—was in the habit of extending Gus a little courtesy from time to time when it came to paying his bar tab.

The bartender opened six bottles of beer. The band members hopped down off the stage and grabbed their drinks, clapping Gus on the back as they went by. So far, so good—he hadn't needed to talk to any of them.

Then the singer picked up his beer and planted himself right in front of Gus. "Thanks," he said, and he proceeded to down the entire bottle in one long, continuous swallow, head tilted back, exposing his long, lean neck.

Usually the most enticing thing about a man was the size of his dick, but now Gus found himself fantasizing about planting kisses—*kisses!*—on this guy's neck. And the singer knew it! When the man lowered the now-empty bottle from his lips, he exhaled slowly, and his eyelids dropped just enough that Gus had no trouble imaging what this guy's face would look like when he came.

"My name's Louis," the singer said. "And you are?"

Gus cleared his throat just to make sure his voice wouldn't come out a squeak. "Augustus Woods," he said. "Gus."

"Well, Gus..." Louis wiped his mouth with the back of his hand. "What about our music?"

"Huh?"

"Your friend." Louis gestured with his head toward Lola. "She said you enjoyed our music. What did you enjoy most?"

Gus swore he'd find a way to get even with Lola, even if it killed him. "Umm...your singing, I guess."

The small smile came back to Louis's lips. "Yeah? Which song? The one where I did this?" Gus winced—he couldn't help it—as Louis let loose with the most god-awful scream Gus had ever heard. "Or my tribute to the songs of the great Elvis Presley?" This time the volume of Louis's scream came down a notch or two, but Gus had no earthly idea which Elvis song Louis was attempting to pay tribute to.

"Yeah, that one," Gus said, hoping he'd picked right. "I like the King."

Something like genuine appreciation stole over the singer's face. "Yeah? He was my idol when I was a kid." When he was a kid. Up close, Gus could see that Louis couldn't be much more than mid-twenties, if that, which made him a good ten years younger than Gus. "I patterned some of my choreography after him," Louis said. "Like this," and he gyrated his hips in a move that would have dislocated a lesser man's spine.

Sensing an opportunity that might not come his way again, Gus screwed up his courage. "You wanna go someplace and talk about the King?"

Heart pounding harder than it had in years, Gus watched

Louis consider the invitation. Behind Louis's back, Lola was giving Gus a double thumbs up and a silly grin.

"Tell you what," Louis finally said, putting the empty beer bottle on the bar. "Pick me up here tomorrow night at seven. We can have dinner, and then see where it goes." Louis's eyes never left Gus's face, but Gus had the feeling Louis knew exactly how hard Gus's cock was. "You up for that?"

"Uh...yeah, I guess so," Gus said.

"Great!" Louis grabbed Gus by the hand and shook. "Tomorrow night then."

Louis hopped back up on stage to help the rest of the band members pack up. Lola grabbed Gus by the elbow and escorted him out of Diamond Pete's.

The cold night air cleared the cobwebs from Gus's head. "What the hell just happened back there?" he asked.

"You got yourself a date," Lola said. "Good for you!"

A date? Dates were for guys looking for a relationship, and that definitely was not Gus.

"I don't date."

"Well, you don't fall in love either, but there's a first time for everything."

"Love? I didn't say anything about love!"

"You didn't have to." Lola swatted Gus in the middle of his forehead with the flat of her hand.

"Ouch! What did you do that for?"

"Just thought I'd wake you up. Tonight you got smacked between the eyes by the love fairy. Love at first sight. I seen it happen often enough. It happens to me all the time, but you're too stubborn to admit it could happen to you too."

Lola was right. Gus was stubborn. He wasn't in love, and he didn't go on dates. He just had a case of bad beer nuts. Tomorrow morning he'd feel better. Tomorrow night he'd meet

Lou-*ee!* at Diamond Pete's and fuck his brains out in the john, then go home and eat dinner *by himself* in front of his television, and that would be that.

Except it wasn't.

Gus spent the entire next day doing nothing but thinking of bedroom-sexy, darkly shadowed eyes, a husky rough voice, that long, lean neck, and those sinful, unruly curls. He went home from work, showered and shaved, and spent the next fifteen minutes deciding what to wear. He finally put on his cleanest jeans and a blue plaid shirt that Lola had once told him made his eyes look bluer.

Eyes look bluer? Gus stared at his reflection in the mirror. His eyes had a definite deer-in-the-headlights look. A light sheen of sweat topped his forehead. "What, am I nuts?" he muttered. His stomach still felt fluttery and nervous. Even his palms were damp. He couldn't blame it on the beer nuts anymore either, but something was definitely wrong with him. It just wasn't love.

"I'm getting senile," Gus said. All this talk of love had him rattled. He patted his hair down, decided it was all Lola's fault, and headed out for Diamond Pete's.

Gus arrived at the bar a good ten minutes early. Pete himself was on bar duty. He took one look at gussied-up Gus and both eyebrows rose halfway up his forehead.

"Don't you say a word," Gus muttered. "Gimme a beer."

"On your tab?" Pete asked.

"Yeah. And hold the nuts."

Louis arrived at five minutes past seven. No tight, black leather pants. No white shirt open to his navel. No eye shadow or eye liner. Just one damn fine-looking man in jeans and a sinfully clingy light blue T-shirt. In fact, Gus decided that Louis just might be the most handsome man he had ever seen in his life.

"Sorry I'm late," Louis said as he slid onto the bar stool next to Gus. "It's one of my least favorable qualities, as my mother used to say." He signaled to Pete for a beer of his own. "Any ideas where you might want to go for dinner?"

Gus realized he hadn't thought that far ahead. "You have a favorite?" he asked, trying not to sound lame.

Louis gave him a genuine grin. "You don't date often, do you?"

Lie, or... "No," Gus admitted. "Guess I'm out of practice." Not that he'd ever been in practice.

"Fair enough." Louis suggested a family diner-type restaurant a half-mile away. Gus was a little disappointed. When he'd thought about this dinner throughout the day, he'd imagined going somewhere with a little more intimate atmosphere.

Much to Gus's surprise, his dinner date with Louis turned out to be the most fun he'd had in a long, long time. Louis was a charming conversationalist. He'd traveled throughout the United States with his band, always playing small, hometown bars like Diamond Pete's. "No place big," Louis said. "At least not yet." He knew more odd local stories than anyone Gus had ever met. Louis used his hands and a wide array of facial expressions when he talked, and Gus got the idea the guy was a natural-born entertainer.

"You always want to be a singer?" Gus asked when the conversation hit a comfortable lag.

Louis nodded. "My mother watched Elvis Presley movies almost constantly when I was little. I think she must have been his biggest fan. She saw him perform live once when she was young. Her eyes lit up whenever she talked about it. I started singing along to his songs when I couldn't have been more than four or five." His grin seemed a little wistful. "She said Elvis might be the king, but I was the crown prince of rock 'n' roll."

"The crown prince, huh?" Somehow the silly title didn't sound so silly when it was applied to Louis.

Louis blushed a little. "Yeah. You know, I don't normally tell people that. Most guys would think I'm an egotistical jerk."

"I don't," Gus said.

"Yeah." Louis looked Gus in the eyes. "I get the feeling you're not most guys."

This time the lag in the conversation felt charged with a pleasant tension. Judging by the tightness in his jeans, Gus wouldn't have to worry about his dick not working anytime in the foreseeable future.

And the funny thing was, the rush of lust Gus felt wasn't the best thing about his evening so far with Louis. Gus hadn't connected—really connected—with another man in a long, long time. Sure, he might bury his dick balls deep in another guy's ass on a fairly regular basis, but that wasn't the kind of connection he meant. Gus felt like he was getting to know Louis, and Gus liked him more and more the longer the evening went on. As much as he could imagine himself fucking Louis, he could also see himself sitting down to dinner on a regular basis with the man. Going for walks, talking about important stuff or about nothing at all. Maybe even catching a movie.

"You like movies?" Gus blurted out.

Louis laughed. "Definitely not like most guys," he said. "And yes, I do like movies. I don't get the opportunity to go often, between rehearsals and performances. I watch most of my movies in motel rooms. Are there any good ones in town?"

Gus said there were, and he paid the check. For the next two hours he sat next to Louis in a dark theater watching the latest big-budget action flick. Gus had no idea what the movie was called, and he didn't follow much of the story. If there even was a story. Gus was too distracted by the feel of Louis's hand in his and the tantalizing warmth of the man's thigh next to his own. Louis had never realized that touching without fucking could feel so good.

Even when they said good night with only a simple, no-tongues-involved kiss, Gus still felt good, if hard enough to cut glass. He went home and took care of himself while fantasizing about Louis and fell asleep with a grin on his face.

Okay, so if this wasn't love, it damn well ought to be.

Gus and Louis dated twice more the same week, and each date ended the same way: a chaste kiss on the lips and a smile from Louis as he walked to his car. Gus, while enjoying the hell out of himself during dinner and holding hands during the movie, was beginning to think that being in love meant having sex with himself instead of with the object of his affection.

"I don't get it," Gus complained to Lola over a beer at Diamond Pete's. Louis had to go to rehearsal, and Lola, like usual, was up for a drink on short notice, provided Gus was buying. "We have a great time, but he doesn't seem interested in getting down to business."

"Well, when you put it like that, I don't blame him," Lola said. "What you have on your hands is a man who wants to be wooed."

"Wooed?"

"Yes. Wooed. He's not one of your backroom boys. Maybe he's saving himself for the right man."

Gus nearly spit out his beer. "Saving himself? You think someone who humps a microphone stand on stage is saving himself?"

Lola paused. "I see your point."

But Gus could see hers too. Only...how did a guy go about wooing another guy? That kind of thing wasn't covered in any big-budget Hollywood action movie Gus had ever seen.

"So what should I do?"

"Flowers are always nice," Lola said.

Gus tried to imagine himself sending Louis flowers. He couldn't. "What else?"

"Candy's traditional."

Louis never even ordered dessert. "Uh-uh."

"Candlelight dinner?"

"We already go to dinner. No candlelight involved."

Lola sighed. "Pathetic. Truly pathetic. What you need is to find something that's special to him and give him that. A special gift, yes, that's what you need," Lola said, warming to the subject. "That kind of thing sticks with a person."

A special gift. Ho, boy. "I'm not exactly made of money, here."

"Did I say 'expensive'? No, I don't think I did. I said 'special.' Even with your thick head, I'm sure you can tell the difference." Lola knocked back the rest of her beer. She might be a girl these days, but Lola still drank like Lonnie.

Gus thought for a few minutes. He thought hard. And came up with absolutely nothing in the way of ideas as to what Louis might think was special. "Aw, hell," he said. "It's probably for the best. He travels with that band of his. Not like he's gonna stick around and keep playing in this place for the rest of his life."

Lola's mouth fell open. "Did I just hear you right? You did some thinking about the long haul with this man?"

Gus blinked. Sure, the words had just poured out of his mouth without a second thought, but he'd never even considered the concept. The long haul. Could he be with the same man for what, the rest of his life? Gus thought about it. And thought some more. Finished his beer. Ordered another one. And came to the conclusion that where Louis was concerned, the answer might just be yes. Provided Gus could figure out a way to be with him in the first place.

Which brought the conversation back around to needing to find the "something special" in order to woo Louis.

"He did say he told me something he never told anybody else," Gus said slowly, thinking back to their conversation about Elvis.

"What?" Lola asked.

Gus shook his head. "Uh-uh," he said, still thinking. "I don't kiss and tell—"

"Since when?"

"—and I for sure am not telling you what he told me."

Lola gave him a long, hard look, then she smiled. A warm, genuine smile. "My man, I am proud of you. Thinking of somebody else's feelings instead of just your own dick." She slid off the bar seat and yanked her too-short, tight little skirt back into place. "I'm gonna go hit on that nice gentleman in the corner. He's been giving me the hairy eyeball all night long, and I bet you a week's wages he ain't never had a taste of anything like me before."

Gus knew better than to take that bet. He said good night to Pete behind the bar and hurried out to his car. He had an idea—finally!—and some work to do before the next time he saw Louis.

In the end, Gus couldn't get everything he wanted together, but he hoped it was enough. Instead of flowers, he arranged for one copy of every Elvis Presley movie available on DVD to be delivered to Louis direct from an online discount store, and he paid extra for overnight shipping. He downloaded three different Elvis songs into his MP3 player and practiced singing along with the King. Gus didn't have anywhere near as good a singing voice as Louis, but he was hoping effort would count for more than end product.

Gus thought about slicking up his hair in an Elvis pompadour, but his hair wasn't full enough or long enough. Besides, he wanted to woo Louis, not creep him out. Elvis impersonators scored high on Gus's personal creep-out meter.

A giant-sized case of nerves set in when Gus knocked on Louis's motel room door. The band had rented rooms for the ten days they'd be in town, and Louis, as lead singer, had his own room.

When Louis opened the door, he was holding the package of DVDs in his hand, and he was scowling. "I'm not sure why you felt it necessary to buy these for me," he said. "The room doesn't have a DVD player and neither do I."

Gus held up the little portable player he'd borrowed from Lola. "Brought one with me."

"Oh." Louis backed away from the door, and Gus took that as an invitation to come in.

The room was simple, like most low-rent motel rooms were. Two double beds took up most of the space. A TV was bolted to the dresser, a lamp bolted to the night stand in between the two beds. The air conditioner chugged away in the window, and ice sat melting in a little plastic ice bucket on the top of the dresser. A battered suitcase, lid closed, sat on the floor between the wall and the bed Louis obviously slept in. Sheet music was spread over the top of the second bed.

Gus felt like an awkward teenager. This had been a bad, bad plan. He might not have ever been in love before, but he had plenty of experience reading a guy's body language. Louis stood on the other side of the still-made bed with his arms crossed in front of him. He wasn't scowling anymore, but even without the scowl Gus read the "Stay the hell away from me" vibe loud and clear. A heavy feeling settled in his chest, and his hands and feet suddenly felt like they weighed a ton.

"Hey, look," Gus said. "You're working and I'm interrupting. Maybe I should just go."

Louis's eyes grew dark. "If that's what you want."

Once again, Gus's mouth took over before his brain kicked in. "It's the last thing I want. I busted my butt trying to do something special for you, but I admit, I'm probably doing it all wrong 'cause I have no idea what I'm doing, and that's just not like me. You can ask Lola."

"Your friend with the big shoulders."

"Yeah."

"The one who said you liked our music."

Gus nodded.

"But you don't, not really."

"I don't know dick about music," Gus said. "I got this little MP3 thing here"—he took the player out of his shirt pocket—"and I put some stuff on it." He shrugged. "I don't have a clue."

Louis took a few tentative steps in Gus's direction, then he seemed to make up his mind. He closed the rest of the distance between them with the same kind of confidence he'd shown striding on stage. "Let me see what you've got here."

Gus handed the player over. Louis scrolled through the short playlist. He paused, one eyebrow lifted. "Love Me Tender"?

Gus stared down at the floor. "Yeah. I just got that. I was gonna sing it for you tonight."

"Sing it for me?"

Couldn't the floor just open up and swallow him whole? It had to be better than standing here in front of a guy he cared about—hell, let's not mince words: the guy he *loved*—and hear, out loud, how silly it all sounded.

"It's the only one that didn't make the dogs howl."

Louis made a funny little sound, halfway between a grunt and a sigh, then the next thing Gus knew, Louis had grabbed his face with both hands and was kissing the stuffing out of him.

Gus knew how to kiss when he had to, but Louis knew how to *kiss*. Gus had never been kissed to the point where he lost track of where he was, but one second he was luxuriating in the full-court press Louis was laying on him, and the next thing he knew, he was on his back with Louis on top of him. Paper rustled on the bed beneath them.

"Wait," Gus managed to get out in between kisses. "Your music. We should—"

"Garbage," Louis said, his voice deep and breathy all at the same time. "Forget about it. Couldn't get it right anyway." Then he went back to kissing Gus, and Gus lost track of himself again.

The next thing he knew, Gus felt his cock being actively and expertly stroked. His shirt was off, his jeans were down around his knees, and Louis was nearly naked except for a pair of boxers that were doing nothing to contain a fairly impressive hard-on.

"How did you do that?" Gus asked.

"What, this?" Louis stroked him hard and finished with a twist of his fist that made Gus groan.

"Oh, man, that was nice, but I meant get me naked without me knowing."

Louis grinned. "It's all in the kissing. I love to kiss."

Gus barely managed to keep from spurting out "I love you" in return. He knew better. He might be in love, but he had no illusions about Louis. When Louis moved on and Gus never saw him again, he might be heartbroken, but at least he would have had one night with the man of his dreams. "Then c'mere and do some more of that again," Gus said instead.

Louis did indeed do more kissing. And not just on the mouth. He kissed Gus on the shoulders and in the little hollow of his throat. On the bend of his elbows and the inside of his thighs. He ran his tongue around the taut muscles of Gus's belly and the hard planes of his chest. Louis kissed Gus on the nipples and on his balls, and finally all over his throbbing cock. He made Gus cum and then made him hard all over again.

When Gus finally found himself buried balls-deep inside Louis, grunting and thrusting and stroking Louis's cock, it was all he could do not to tell Louis how much better it felt to fuck—no, make love—when he was in love. Before it had always been about fucking for as long as he could just because he got off on making the other guy cum first. This time it wasn't about Gus getting off at all; it was about making Louis feel as good as he possibly could. When Louis finally came in Gus's hand, the mere feel of his body shuddering and bucking made Gus cum too.

Afterward, Gus didn't know what to expect. Was he supposed to stay? Get his shit and leave? He had no clue.

Louis rolled over and their eyes met. Louis's hair was a mess, but his face looked radiant. "I'll have you know, I don't normally do this." He placed a small peck of a kiss on the tip of Gus's nose. "I don't get involved. I'm always moving from place to place, and the most I ever allow myself is a quick fuck in a john or something. But you're different." He brushed his hand along the top of Gus's hair. "You gave me Elvis."

Gus didn't know how to take that. His "special" gift seemed manipulative, and he didn't like that. "You went to bed with me because I sent you Elvis movies?"

"No. I went to bed with you because you cared enough about me to know how much I'd like them. It was the feeling behind the gift. I saw that feeling in your eyes the first night. I kept you at arm's length because I wasn't sure if it was real or if you were one of those guys who can turn it on in an instant just to get in my pants so they can say they fucked a rock 'n' roll singer."

Gus realized what it must be like to be someone like Louis, never sure if a guy was coming on to you for who you were or what you were. "Not just any singer," Gus said. "The Crown Prince of Rock 'n' Roll."

Louis laughed. "Careful. With flattery like that, I might exercise my princely authority and make you sing."

"It wouldn't be pretty."

"You said you didn't make the dogs howl."

"My neighbor's dogs. They were outside. It's a quiet song."

Louis laughed again, then he kissed Gus. Not chastely, nor a mere peck on the lips, but not with all consuming passion either. This was a kiss filled with feelings that couldn't be spoken, not just yet.

The kiss made Gus wonder if he was the only one who'd fallen in love at first sight. Louis admitted to doing things with Gus that he didn't do with anyone else. That had to count for something, right?

Augustus Woods didn't think love was a bunch of hooey, not anymore. In fact, he was kind of hopeful about the whole thing. Sure, Louis traveled a lot, but they could work things out. That's what happened when people were in love. They worked things out. Love made a guy think that after all those years of empty fucking, things would work out for him too.

As Lola would say, it was about damn time.

IN A CLEARING

Rob Rosen

B en stopped his horse at the stream and hopped down to
the ground, stroking the great steed's flank as she lapped at
the cool, fresh water. The mare's body trembled at his touch,
a contented snort rumbling through the surrounding oaks and
pines. "Good girl," he cooed, his neck craning from right to
left, taking in the unfamiliar stretch of forest he now found
himself in. He tied the horse to a sturdy tree, and added, "Be
right back, girl."

He heard rushing water and followed it to the base of a
majestic waterfall, its white waters burbling over the side of
a granite outcropping before pooling in the crystal-clear pond
below. The sun's rays dappled across its surface. Standing dead
center, torso just above the water, stood a naked man. Ben
groaned at the sight of him and ducked behind an old fir.

The stranger was washing his broad chest, the suds forming
within the dense matting of ebony hair that grew in the wide
expanse between his jutting nipples before trailing down his

finely etched stomach. Instinctively, Ben's hand reached inside his leather riding pants, his cock already thick, leaking. He gave a squeeze, a tug, a near-silent moan.

The stranger glanced up, eyes blue as the sky on a hot, summer's day, dazzling beneath the brilliant midday sun. A spark lit from within Ben's belly, spreading like brushfire before exploding up his spine, a million goose bumps riding down both arms. His cock was now as hard as any of the overhead branches as he stepped away from the tree and into the clearing beside the pond, his fine leather boots coming to a stop where the water met the land.

"You there," he managed, his voice suddenly raspy, throat as dry as a burning timber. "Is the water warm enough for a dip?"

The stranger jumped, and his thick black bush was suddenly visible above the water, the base of his shaft appearing and then disappearing. He squinted, eyes taking in Ben from head to toe, a nervous tic lifting his eyebrow a tad northward. "Warm enough," came the throaty response, followed by a nod of his head.

"And is there room enough for two?" added Ben, arms akimbo, a broad smile stretched across his face.

The stranger turned his head from side to side. "And many more, I would think," he replied, playing with the tuft of hair that sprouted from his dimpled chin. And then he watched in silence as Ben kicked off his boots, then undid his vest and placed it on the ground. Ben opened his undershirt, one button at a time, revealing inch by glorious inch the body he knew to be lean and tan, until the shirt lay beside the vest.

"Good day for a swim," Ben noted, looking up, their eyes locking as Ben reached for the clasp at the top of his riding trousers.

"If you say so," replied the stranger, a frown suddenly

appearing, the light from behind his magnificent orbs of blue briefly dimming, flickering like a fading flame.

Ben pushed down on the leather, the pants gathering at his bare feet before they were kicked off, leaving him standing at the water's edge, naked as the day he was born, cock semi-turgid, though gratefully no longer at full mast. He dipped a toe in and smiled. "Why so glum, friend? The water is just about perfect." In he strode, sending ripples in his wake as he approached the center of the pond, until both men stood a foot apart, face to handsome face.

The stranger sighed, head cast downward. "Today is my wedding day."

Ben forced a smile and reached out his hand. "Ah, that is good news then, friend. Congratulations."

The stranger looked up and grabbed for the hand, the shake weak. Still, with flesh now pressed to flesh, that spark in Ben's belly grew to a blazing inferno, raging through him with a force that nearly knocked him over. The stranger's chest suddenly rose and fell, his mouth agape, eyes once again sparkling like sapphires. "Thank you," came the man's reedy reply. "I suppose."

The handshake lingered, neither breaking contact just yet, the gap between them closing even further. "I am called Ben."

"William," said the stranger.

"I take it this marriage is not to your liking then, William?"

The sigh returned. "No. Arranged by my father. My bride's family manages the farm to our west. Our marriage would strengthen their bargaining abilities with the surrounding villages."

"I see," said Ben, with a nod. "And this woman of yours, is she homely, hunched over, missing a limb, her teeth? Covered with moles, is she?"

William laughed, the sound to Ben's ears like a breeze rustling through the trees. "No, she is, by all accounts, quite fair."

Ben returned the laughter in kind. "But not by your account, I take it?" He stared at William, an edge now apparent to his voice, both of them locking eyes once more, the fire now at a fevered pitch.

William paused for a moment, clearly collecting his thoughts. "She's not what I was, what I was hoping for, I'd say." He exhaled, sharply, the smile managing a triumphant return.

"I see," Ben repeated, grabbing for the thick, brown mane that hung down to his shoulders. "Is her hair blond while you prefer dark?"

William reached his hand up and out, his fingers wrapping around Ben's locks, a flush of crimson riding up his neck before spreading across both cheeks. "In fact, yes, that is so."

Ben released his hair and touched his index finger to his eyelid. "Her eyes are blue and you prefer brown?"

William nodded, repeating Ben's actions, a gentle stroke to a fluttering lid, a glide down a scruffy cheek. "Just as you say, friend."

Ben moved his palm out and rested it above William's chest, feeling his heart thumping madly from within. "Her bosom is not ample enough for you?"

William set his hand on Ben's chest, his finger brushing a sensitive nipple, causing Ben to shudder, his knees to buckle. "Hers is like a robin's breast, friend. Not nearly half as abundant as your own, I would say."

And then last, staring down, his cock jutting out, resting atop the water, Ben asked, "And she lacks one of these?"

William too glanced down, the smile big and bright, teeth white as a cloud. He reached down beneath the water, cupping Ben's hefty balls in his farm-worked hands. "Nor these, friend."

"Sad," said Ben, his grin as sly as a fox's.

"Very," agreed William. "Nor lips as pink and full as your own," he added, the gap at last closed, one mouth brushing the other before colliding, two tongues entwined, snaking and coiling as Ben pulled William in, chest to chest, cock to cock, hands roaming from north to south.

"Shall I help you forget your troubles then, William?" Ben whispered, their foreheads pressed together as they tried to catch their breaths. "A wedding present, shall we say?"

The sigh rumbled through one body and out the other. "Is this not present enough?" he asked, reaching down for a stroke on Ben's massive tool.

Ben groaned. "Wait until you see what I can do with such a gift, William."

"A memory to keep me going?"

The groan turned to a laugh. "And going and going, I would think."

William nodded. "Then yes, Ben, I'd like that present. Very much indeed."

"It will be a memory for each of us, friend, to keep us both going during the long days ahead."

William grabbed Ben's hand and led him to the waterfall, their bodies wading through the clear pond, sweat now trickling down their backs, cocks sloshing from side to side. He stopped in front of the cascade and turned to Ben with a smile as big as the moon's. Without a word he continued forward, his body disappearing within the heavy flow of water, pulling Ben with him, until they stood behind the falls. William led them into a concealed cave. The sound of the water bounced off the rocky walls, loud as thunder, the smell of damp moss rushing up their nostrils.

"Now then," said William, holding on tight to his partner, lips nuzzled to neck, fingers tweaking a rigid nipple. "Let us see what this rod of yours can do."

Ben moaned, the sound swirling all around them, barely discernable above the roar of the wall of rushing water at their backs. He pulled away, hands raised before landing with a *thwack* atop William's hairy chest, a flash of red rising through. "Is that what you would like, good groom?" He grinned a mischievous grin.

William lifted his own hands up, crashing them down atop Ben's brawny chest, a second time, a third, then a spank across a stony ab. "A present is a present, friend. It is bad manners to offer one only to take it back."

Ben gently smacked the underside of William's shaft, sending his cock swaying. "Bad manners, is it?" He chuckled. "Heaven forbid." And then he swung William around and forced him to the ground, knees atop the damp moss, pushing him forward. The man was now down on all fours, legs spread wide, a pink, crinkled, hair-rimmed hole winking out, balls dangling low. Ben moaned at the glorious sight of it. He'd seen fine art in the castle that couldn't hold a candle to this.

Again his hands lifted, palms crashing down on two alabaster cheeks, once, twice, the white turning red, moans turning to groans, groans to whimpers as William's legs spread even wider, his arm reaching back, fingers rubbing his hole. "Perhaps another whack here then, friend."

Ben nodded, fingers pressed in tight together before the smack was administered, a quick swat, then another, William's back arching at each point of contact, massive balls swaying to and fro, cock dripping now. "Like that?" Ben rasped, leaning in, taking a deep whiff of the hole, the aroma of musk and sweat wafting up his nose, the scent intoxicating.

"Switch a tongue for a digit, I would think. Then a cock for a tongue," came the groaned response.

Ben gave a lick, the tongue in question running rings around the offered portal, his hands grabbing for William's balls for a tug and a pull, a twist and a yank. "As you wish, friend," he said, diving in, the slick appendage pushing its way inside, sweat pouring down, putting the falls to shame. And then, when William was good and wet, Ben added, "Now a cock for a tongue, just as you asked for."

William grabbed for his cheeks, pulling them apart, stretching the hole out. "Deep as you can go," he groaned.

"Oh, my pleasure, friend," said Ben, spitting down onto his thick cock, a gob onto the twitching hole before he slapped his prick down against it, easing it in, gentle as a lamb, a bolt of lightning shooting up his spine as he smacked William's ass and then slid his prick inside.

William arched his back and inhaled, sharply, clenching his ring before he exhaled and allowed the invasion. "Mmm," he moaned, the sound whipping around the cave.

"Mmm," Ben echoed, more and more of his cock disappearing, until his balls brushed up against ass, the pulsing head butting up against muscle. On his knees now, he rested his cheek atop William's broad, tan shoulder, his hand reaching around to stroke his massive club of a dick. The flesh pulsed in his grip.

"I fear my bride is no longer marrying a virgin," said William, laughing.

"Your fear should be that your bride will have a cock as big as mine. Then and only then will she ever know about your loss of virginity." Ben laughed as well, torso again ramrod straight up as he eased his prick out, all the way, in an audible *pop*, before shoving it in again, deep, deep in. Then out again, *pop*, the thrust harder this time, in, all the way, both of them sweat-drenched from the exertion.

"W…w…ait," managed William. "Flip me around so that I can watch as you fuck me."

Again the *pop*, William's body flung over like nothing more than a rag doll's, two palms smacking down on the wet chest below. Then legs spread out, ankles on shoulders, the shove in again, their faces an inch apart. "Better, friend?" groaned Ben, with a kiss so intense that they both saw stars before their eyes.

"Better," cried William, when at last they came up for air.

Ben sank his cock in, grabbing on to the rock-hard shaft pointing up at him, stroking it rapid-fast as he thrust and pumped his prick in and out, in and out, slamming away until William's hefty, hairy balls started their inevitable rise.

"Close," howled William.

"Closer," grunted Ben, a final deep shove inside, his body tensed, every muscle taut as he shot, filling William's tight hole with ounce after ounce of molten-hot cum. And still his hand pumped away down below, William's cock erupting a split second later, his white, pungent load spewing up and out, dousing Ben's belly and chest before dripping down. Both men were gasping, sweat flinging off of them.

Spent, Ben popped his prick out and collapsed on top of William, a kiss replaced by a hundred more, eyes open, locked, William's arms encircling Ben's drenched body, fingers digging into flesh.

"A fine present for my wedding," William panted.

"Indeed," agreed Ben, stroking William's hair.

Both men showered in the rush of the falls, hand in hand, savoring their few remaining moments together. Then clean, they once more stood face to face. "Good luck today, friend," offered Ben, his hands around William's waist, those blue eyes drilling in, a swarm of butterflies suddenly fluttering around inside his gut.

"I've fresh ran out of luck, it would seem," lamented William. "My family truly needs this merging."

"And you, William, what is it that you need?"

William smiled, mouth on mouth again. He pointed to the moss, to the ground, to the place they'd risen from. "*That* merging," he whispered, exhaling down Ben's throat.

And with a final perfect kiss, they returned for their clothes, and then, sadly, parted ways, William back to his farm, Ben to his horse, both men gazing over their shoulders until the other was clean out of sight.

"Did you have a good afternoon, girl?" Ben asked the mare, hand brushing her silver mane. She snorted and rocked her head. "Yes, me as well." He smiled, his mind lost in thought. "But now on to more pressing matters. We have little time to spare, I'm afraid."

And so the day passed quickly, the sun beginning its gradual descent as the wedding party took shape. A small gathering formed between the two farms, both families milling about, the bride and groom at the ready, plus a smattering of village folk, the priest off to the side. Garlands of white flowers festooned the nearby grove of tree. All were smiling. All but one.

No one noticed Ben as he slipped in at the back of the wedding party. The priest walked up and stood before the soon to be husband and wife. The ceremony began, finally reaching the point Ben had been waiting for. "If anyone here today objects to this union, speak now or forever hold your peace."

All heads turned in surprise as Ben boomed, "I object!" A great clamoring arose among the throng, all eyes on him.

"On what grounds?" asked the priest, his face suddenly red, hands wringing.

Ben smiled, his eyes locked on to a blue so deep as to take one's very breath away. "On the grounds that this groom does not love his bride."

William's father spoke up next. "What business is this of

yours, stranger?" he asked, face even redder than the priest's.

Ben looked briefly to the man. "I gave your son a wedding present earlier today," he replied, his smile growing even brighter. "But I've come to realize that it was insufficient."

William moved in and stood by Ben's side. "Please, you can't do this," he whispered.

Ben nodded, and whispered back. "Oh, but I must, friend." And then he looked again to the father. "This marriage, it will benefit you financially, I take it?"

The father, too, nodded. "Of course it will, stranger. The king demands his rent for this land we find ourselves on."

The father of the bride piped in next. "And our land, as well."

"Aye," said William's father. "If we can turn a higher profit on our crops by joining both farms as one, then the king will make his rent and we will have silver in our pockets."

Again Ben nodded, two piece of parchment in his hand, the ones he'd retrieved the hour prior. "Then my present, good sir," he said, handing him the parchments.

The father looked in stunned disbelief at what was handed to him. "The king has absolved us of our rent?"

Ben's nod turned to a shake, head moving back and forth. "Not the king, but his son."

"The prince?" it was asked. "Prince Benjamin?"

William sucked in his breath. "Benjamin?" He looked into Ben's eyes, the two again united as one. "Ben?" he asked, lips quivering before the smile formed.

"Did I neglect to inform you of this before?" he asked.

William leaned in, and whispered, "We had more pressing matters to attend to, *Your Highness*." And then he turned to his father. "As Prince Benjamin says, Father, I do not love this woman."

"And this union is no longer necessary," added Ben.

"And that," agreed William, readily.

The two fathers stared at one another and shrugged. Even the bride looked relieved. "Fine then," the priest said. "The wedding will no longer take place."

William's smile instantly grew as wide as Ben's. And then he stared down, a third piece of parchment proffered. "What is this?" he asked, his eyes scanning the document.

"The clearing," said the prince. "It is now in your name, to do with as you please." He said this as he mounted his steed, his hand held down, asking for William's. William grabbed for it, flesh once again on flesh, the fire in Ben's belly burning right on though.

And with that, the two of them galloped off into the sunset.

Well, into the sunset via a certain clearing, of course.

THE PRINCE AND THE PLUMBER

J. L. Merrow

Right, Tom, got a new one for you."

I grabbed for the docket, only to have Nige pull it back out of reach. Tosser. "So are you going to give it to me, or what?"

Nige leaned back in his chair and swiveled it 'round a bit. I thought about suggesting something else he could sit and swivel on. "Ground rules, Tom," he said, tapping his nose. "This isn't your ordinary client. Piss this bloke off and I'll have your bollocks for breakfast."

I'd like to see him try. "Nige, you say that about half the jobs you send me on. What is it this time, Buckingham Palace? Prince Charles need his drains unblocked?"

"Close enough. This is your genuine Hollywood royalty, here. Biggest client we got. I want an assurance from you that anything you see there ain't going nowhere else. If I open up my paper tomorrow to see you telling the world about the state of his bloody bog I'll be shoving a plunger up where the sun don't shine."

"Ooh, promises, promises." I cocked a hip and blew him a kiss. It winds Nige up something chronic when I go all gay on him. "So who is it? Guy Richie need his plughole cleared of Madge's extensions?" They're a bitch, those hair things. What gets me is sometimes the client wants them back, even if they've been halfway down the soil pipe with Christ knows what.

"Oh, much bigger than that." Nige made a gun out of his fingers and shot me point blank. I didn't bother to die. "His name is Finn. Brendan Finn."

Okay, I'll admit it. I was impressed, although not by Nige's bloody awful impressions. "The Bond bloke? Are you pissing me about? You're telling me I got a callout from the new James Bond?"

"Uh-huh, and you'd better get your little Octopussy over there before he gets pissed off waiting and lets his fingers do the bloody walking. Here's the address." Finally, he gave me the docket.

"Cheers, Nige!" I snatched it out of his hand and was out the door and in the van in two seconds flat. M would have been proud of me. I thought about programming the Satnav but hey, would James Bond have done that?

Seconds later (all right, twenty minutes or so, after I took a wrong turn round Holland Park) I was pulling up in front of a modest-looking Kensington townhouse. Didn't look much like it was home to one of the hottest (and I mean that in every sense of the word) new actors on the British scene. I mean, who the hell had heard of Brendan Finn before they cast him as the new Bond? But now, with the film due out in the summer, he wasn't just hot property, he was practically radioactive.

And okay, Daniel Craig looked pretty damn good in those swimming trunks, but Brendan? I'd seen the trailers and drooled over the publicity shots, and he was something else. Six foot four of lean, sculpted muscle and handsome-yet-ruthless features. They'd gone back to basics when casting this Bond: dark hair, blue-gray eyes, and a wicked cruel mouth. He'd love you and leave you, this Bond would—but bloody hell, you'd enjoy it while it lasted. I shivered at the thought. And now I was going to meet him. In the flesh.

Maybe Brendan had been about to have a shower when the pipe sprung a leak? Maybe he'd come to the door wrapped in a skimpy little towel, and when he showed me upstairs to the bathroom it'd accidentally fall right off that gorgeous arse....

Or maybe I'd just earn myself a bollocking from Nige if I spent any longer sitting in the van fantasizing instead of getting out and doing my job. And anyway, what were the chances Brendan Finn would deal with his own plumbing emergencies? Ten to one it'd be a pissed off PA who'd hover round getting on my tits all morning and then complain about the bill. I sighed, grabbed my toolkit and went and knocked on the door.

When it opened, I nearly fell off the front step. It was Brendan all right, but he seemed...different, somehow, in the flesh.

Good, different. The hair was longer, more tousled, like he'd just rolled out of bed. Instead of being twisted into a sneer, his mouth was curved into a welcoming smile, and those eyes seemed brighter and softer. "Oh, hello," he said, and his voice— that was the one thing that was just the same as in the trailers. Cultured without being too posh and with a warmth to it that went straight to my groin. "Are you the plumber?"

"That's me. Tom Canty. That's with an 'a,' by the way. You can look it up; I'm in the book." I cleared my throat to stop all the babbling and held out a hand without thinking. He shook it briefly but firmly. Oh, my God. I'd touched James Bond. Was that allowed? "I hear you've got a leak that wants sorting," I managed to say without my voice cracking.

"Yes, that's right. It's in the airing cupboard. Come in," he added, moving back to let me in. Right. Just an ordinary bloke, letting in the plumber. I could handle this. I took a firmer grip of my toolbox, seeing as the hand holding it had gone a bit sweaty, and stepped over the threshold.

There were a couple of packing boxes in the hall. "Moving in or moving out?" I asked, wiping my feet on the mat.

"Oh, moving in. Just bought this place." The smile turned crooked. "You'd have thought I could get through the first month without anything needing fixing."

"Let me guess—your other home is a Hollywood mansion?"

Brendan grinned. "Not exactly. More like a Balham bedsit. I'm a bit new to the business of having some money."

"Poor starving actor? You should get a proper job, mate." We both laughed, and I started to relax a bit. Even James Bond was just another bloke, after all.

A world-famous, rich, and incredibly shaggable bloke, yeah, but still, just a bloke.

Brendan was fully dressed, but you can't have everything. He looked good anyhow, in his faded jeans and Ireland rugby shirt. Made me think longing thoughts about scrums and showers after the game. "You play?" I asked as we skirted the crates.

"Play?" God, he sounded polite. I felt like a right tit.

"Rugby." I sort of waved in the direction of the shirt.

Thankfully, this time he got it. "Oh—not so much. Not any more." He gave me a wry look. "The film company seemed a bit concerned about the prospect of a leading man with no front teeth and a broken nose."

I couldn't blame them. Still I reckoned if anyone could carry it off, he could. "What, the amount of times James Bond gets into fights?" I said with a grin. "If you ask me, it'd just add a bit of realism."

"Realism and James Bond?" He had the eyebrow thing down pat, which was thankfully the only way he resembled Roger Moore in the slightest. "Aren't those two mutually exclusive?" Bloody hell. Gorgeous *and* a sense of humor about himself. Why the hell was this guy single? Course, just because the papers said he was single, didn't mean he really was. Maybe he had Keira Knightley waiting in bed for him.

"Now you're spoiling it for me," I said, following him up the stairs, which incidentally gave me a bloody marvelous view of his arse. "I bet you'll be telling me next you didn't really leap out of that airplane, land on the helicopter's tail, and fight the bad guy while dodging the rotors."

He laughed. "There may have been an element of technical wizardry involved."

"You ought to watch out. Next thing you know you'll be out of a job—they'll just computer-generate the whole bloody thing and not bother with the actors." I was starting to relax a bit too much, I reckoned. But he took it all right.

"Luckily for me, I'll always have waiting on tables to fall back on. Here we are." He waved me into a bedroom that was obviously unused and opened up the airing cupboard.

As expected, the bottom of it was an inch-deep in soggy towels and the pipes were dripping wet. Well, it would have been way too much to hope that he'd got me here under false pretences. "Got another towel, mate?" I asked, my head stuck in the cupboard. "I want to dry it up a bit, see where it's coming from."

Didn't take me long to see what was wrong. I was about to do the pursed-lips-it's-gonna-cost-you thing, but then I remembered this was Brendan Finn, and even if he was new to the film star gig he still probably had more millions than I'd had hot dinners. "You're going to need a new valve on that. Don't worry, I've got one in the van. Won't be a tick."

I leapt down those stairs like I had the KGB on my tail, slowing my pace a bit when it occurred to me just how embarrassing it'd be to break an ankle in front of James Bond. I mean, here's a man who leaps out of airplanes and fights deadly villains for a living, and me not able to get down a flight of stairs without serious injury? Not that Brendan Finn actually was James Bond, of course. He might be a total wuss in real life.

Couldn't see it, mind.

Be a bugger if he was, though, I thought as I rummaged through the crap in the back of the van and tried to find the valve I was after. I mean, imagine playing the ultimate hard man, and inside you're terrified of heights and spiders? It had to put a lot of pressure on a bloke. In bed, and all—James Bond's supposed to be the ultimate lover, so any girl getting frisky with Brendan Finn was bound to have certain expectations. 'Course, not that it was necessarily girls he liked to get frisky with. For all I knew, he was as bent as a bloody S-bend.

Yeah, right. Cast a poof as James Bond? Half the country would be up in arms, and the director would be burned in effigy. That's if he was lucky, and they didn't burn him for real. I grinned to myself. It'd be well cool, though. Would they get him a male Moneypenny to flirt with? I reckoned Gareth Whatshisface would be a shoo-in for the part, especially now they'd killed off Ianto in *Torchwood*, fuck you very much Russell Davies.

I finally unearthed the valve and legged it back to the house.

"Can I get you a cup of tea?" Brendan asked as I reached the top of the stairs.

"Thanks, that'd be great." I kept my voice cool. Not a hint of Oh-my-God-James-Bond-is-making-me-tea. I wondered how much I'd get for it if I bunged it in a travel mug and sold it on eBay. Not that I would, mind. I was going to savor this one.

"White?"

"Yeah, but no sugar."

"Watching your weight? You don't look to me like you need to," he said with a smile, his eyes traveling down my body, and just for a moment, just for one second my heart skipped a beat. Was he eyeing me up?

But when his eyes came back up to meet mine, there was just this bland, polite smile on his face. "I'll go and put the kettle on," he said, not a hint of anything in his voice.

I shook my head as he disappeared. Wishful bloody thinking, that was my problem.

I unpacked the new valve—no point starting before I was sure it'd fit—and got out my tools. "I'm going to have to drain your hot water tank," I called down the stairs, but I wasn't sure if he heard me over the sound of the kettle. Didn't really matter. I turned the taps in the bathroom full on, then wondered if he had an en-suite. Probably. Most of these houses had been modernized like that; it was a plumber's wet dream.

The bedroom door was shut, so I knocked loudly in case Keira was a heavy sleeper and then went in. No Keira. Actually, Brendan's bedroom looked a lot like mine. Same half-arsed attempt to make the bed, same balled-up socks on the floor.

Same gay porn shoved half under the pillow.

I stared. No. Really?

I was almost certain it was a vintage edition of *Bound and Gagged*. I moved closer to the bed, pulled by the magnetic tug of the square inch of flesh and rope that was all I could see. It had to be something else. Didn't it?

Sod it. I pulled the magazine out from under the pillow and goggled at the photo on the front. I didn't need to look at the title to know I'd been right, which was good because my eyes didn't seem to want to shift from all that naked flesh, trussed up and ready. The boy on the front was a bit too young for my tastes, but he bore a passing resemblance to Brendan Finn, so he wasn't all bad. I wouldn't have kicked him out of bed, put it that way.

And with those knots, he'd have been physically incapable of kicking me, or doing a right lot else except awaiting my very great pleasure.... Damn. I had to stop thinking like this. It'd be bloody embarrassing facing Brendan with a stiffy.

That little problem sorted itself out swiftly as the bedroom door opened without warning. I looked up into the eyes of a very pissed-off Brendan Finn. Except right then he looked a hell of a lot more like James Bond. I swear, if he'd had a Walther PPK at that moment, I'd have been a dead man. "What the hell are you doing in here?"

"Sorry mate, I—"

"I think you'd better go."

"But I haven't—"

"Please just leave. My solicitor will be in touch."

Shit. Shit, shit, shit. "Look, I didn't mean to—"

"*Will you get out?*"

It wasn't what he said, or how he said it, that made me give up and leave.

It was the look in those eyes—bleak as winter, and twice as cold.

"You fucking stupid wanker," Nige said the minute I walked into the office. "Couldn't resist the chance to sniff his bloody undies?"

I slumped into the chair opposite him. "I was trying to drain his bloody tank, that was all." I was too hacked off to even give a nod to the double entendre. "How was I to know he kept his porn on display?"

"His porn? Oh, for fuck's sake! Is that all? The way that

bloody lawyer of his was talking about invasion of privacy I thought he'd found you prancing around trying his Calvin Kleins on for size!" Nige leered at me. "What was it—hardcore BDSM? Girls with whips and blokes in nappies? Or are we talking the real nasty stuff?"

I shrugged. If Brendan had given me a chance, I'd have told him his secret was safe with me. "Nothing much. Just the usual." For blokes like me, that was. And Brendan, as it turned out. "So I s'pose you'll be wanting me to clear the van out."

"What?"

"Unless you're giving it to me in lieu of notice." More likely to run me over with it, I'd have thought.

"What the fuck are you on about?"

"How about all that stuff you were saying this morning? How you'd have my arse on a plate if I pissed this bloke off?"

"First, Tom, I want nothing, and I mean *nothing*, to do with that pansy arse of yours, either on a plate or off it, and second, you think I'd let some tosspot lawyer tell me what to do? I told that git where to stuff his bloody lawsuit. Now, take these dockets, get out there and pull your bloody finger out. I ain't paying you to sit around in my office looking pretty."

"Nige, mate, I could kiss you!" I was boneless with relief.

He shuddered. "Do that and I will fire you. Now piss off, will you? I got a business to run here."

That's where I thought it would end. My one meeting with Brendan Finn, 007. Licensed to get really pissed off when he found anyone fingering his porn.

Except it kept preying on my mind—because let's face it, it had to be preying on his. And yeah, maybe he was living a lie, but bloody hell, could you blame him? These days, you can be a character actor and be openly gay. You can be a straight leading man who plays a gay character, and everyone says how fucking brave you are.

But actually be gay, and expect people to accept you as a leading man? As James Bond, womanizer extraordi-fucking-naire? Brendan Finn had been plucked from obscurity to play the role, and if it came out he was queer he'd be back there sooner than he could say Q.

So I knew I had to do something. Just—what? That was the problem. I thought about writing to him, but even I was bright enough to realize that a letter reading *Dear Brendan, don't worry, I won't tell anyone you're a poof, love Tom* was likely to cause more problems than it solved. I mean, he probably had people to open his mail for him—although come to think of it, he'd been pretty hands-on with the plumbing emergency. Still, what if it got lost in the post? In my experience, the chance of something like that happening is in direct proportion to the amount of excrement that'll impact on the air conditioning.

Which is why, three days later, I was knocking on his door once more.

Brendan opened it himself. Wasn't he ever going to get himself an entourage? There was a moment's stillness. When he finally spoke, his voice was cold. "What do you want?"

See, this is when I started to get a bit tetchy. Here I was, on a mission of bloody mercy, and he's acting like I've come demanding hush money. I mean, obviously he didn't know yet what I was going to say, but benefit of the doubt, anyone? "You know what your problem is?" I said. "You think it's all about you, that's what. I could have lost my bloody job after your sodding lawyer rang up my boss! All because you didn't give me a chance to explain."

Brendan's jaw dropped. "Explain?" he hissed. "You were in my bedroom, rifling through my things!"

"One sodding magazine! And I only picked it up to see if it was the same one I've got back home. Which it was, by the way, so I ain't going to be throwing any bloody stones, am I?"

For a moment there he looked a bit—I dunno, startled? Soon got over it, though. "You shouldn't have been in there in the first place. You had no right—"

"Yeah, well, you had no right siccing a bloody lawyer on my boss. Haven't you ever heard of innocent until proven guilty? If you'd let me get a word in edgewise I'd have told you I wasn't going to go running to the press or nothing! And I was in your bloody bedroom because I needed to turn your sodding tap on, all right?" Shit. I was standing on James Bond's doorstep, having a bloody hissy fit. If he'd been a real spy, I'd have been waking up next day halfway down the Thames in a concrete overcoat, while he made some smart-arse remark about me plumbing the depths.

Seemed like the "doorstep" bit had occurred to Brendan, too. He sent a couple of nervous glances across toward the neighbors. "We'd better continue this inside."

But I'd had enough. "Nothing to continue. See this mouth? Zipped. So call off the bloody lawyer, all right? I'll see you around." In the very unlikely event he ever wanted me to fix his pipes again. I turned and walked down the path.

"Tom?" I heard him say as I reached the gate, but I didn't look round, just got in the van and drove off.

So that should have been where it ended. Case closed. Chalk it up to experience. Except next night, when I got home, there was a bouquet of bleeding flowers waiting on the doorstep, with a note that just said, "Sorry." And when I got in to work next day, not in the best of moods because I'd been sneezing all night from the pollen, Nige gave me a funny look.

"What?" I said.

"That is the question, innit? I only had another call from
Brendan Finn's lawyer, didn't I? The bastard's apologized, and
says the check's in the post."

"Check? What check?" If this was hush money I had half a
mind to go straight 'round and tell him where he could shove it,
that and his flowers both.

"What check? What check, he asks? This ain't a bloody
charity. Just because he never let you finish the job doesn't mean
he don't owe us for your time."

"You still sent him a bill? Bloody hell, Nige, you got a
nerve!"

"Worked, though, din't it? Right. You got a toilet in South
Ken, and a mixer tap in Holland Park...."

I spent the day doing odds and sods—bread and butter jobs,
nothing fancy. Left me plenty of time to think. Only trouble was,
I didn't know what to think. The mixer tap turned out to be a
minor soap actor—plumber to the stars, that's me—who talked
to me like I'd just crawled out of her bloody drains. She didn't
offer me a cup of tea even after I'd spent half an hour under her
bath trying to chip through twenty years' worth of limescale.

Not like a certain very bankable film star who'd sent me
flowers the night before.

Which reminded me I needed to bin them when I got home.
Bloody hay fever. I never quite got round to it, though. See,
when I got back that night, there was something else waiting on
the doorstep.

It wasn't flowers.

It was Brendan Finn, wearing a battered leather jacket and a
nervous expression.

Nervous?

"Tom," he said, and stopped.

"Yeah, Brendan?" I answered, seeing as we were apparently on first-name terms.

"I, ah, wanted to apologize to you. For jumping to the wrong conclusion. And the, well, the phone call." He shifted from one foot to the other like his designer shoes were giving him gyp. "Um...just so you know, it wasn't really a lawyer. I haven't got one. I, er, had a bit part as a barrister in *The Bill* once, so I just sort of got into character...."

I had to laugh. "You tosser! You mean, all this time I was shitting myself, and it was just another Oscar-winning performance?"

Brendan made a face like he'd just caught his nuts in his zip, but his fingers stopped drumming on his thigh. "I thought the number on the card was your mobile. I didn't realize it wasn't you on the phone until it was too late, and then I just had to carry on. I swear, if I'd known it was your boss and I was putting your job in danger...."

M would have been horrified. Hell, she'd have booked him in for psychiatric care, and not in the bloody community either. James Bond, apologizing to a plumber? Admitting he'd pretended to be his own lawyer?

Then again, it'd been proved pretty bloody conclusively that Brendan Finn was not, in fact, James Bond. Just a bloke. And all right, he was rich and famous and so bloody gorgeous it made you want to weep, but still. Just a bloke. One who I had a couple of things in common with, as it happened. I smiled. "Want to come in? I was going to make some pasta, if you're hungry."

He blinked. And then he smiled back. "I love pasta."

"How did you find me, by the way?" I asked as I let him in and did a quick scan for anything too embarrassing, like week-old dirty socks.

"Tom Canty? With an 'a'? You're in the book, remember?"

Bloody hell. He'd remembered that? Must be all that practice learning lines.

I gave him fettuccine with aubergines and tomatoes, and grilled chicken on the side, because he's an actor, he's got to watch his weight, right? Opened a bottle of Sainsbury's Chianti, too. I've got class, me.

"That was fantastic," Brendan sighed as he scooped up the last of the food with his fork.

"You've got sauce on your chin," I told him, and used a finger to wipe it clean. Brendan drew in his breath sharply.

"I miss this," he said, turning away. "Just…dinner with a friend. That kind of thing. Not having to live up to the image."

My eyes narrowed. "Is that what we are, then? Friends?"

"Um," he said.

"Thought you actor types were supposed to have a way with words?"

He gave me a grin, his hair flopping over one eyebrow. "I'm useless without a script, I'm afraid."

"Oh, yeah? Maybe I should write one for you," I told him, heat flaring in my belly.

"What would it say?" he asked, looking straight at me with eyes so bloody blue it made it hard to think.

"Oh, I don't know. Something like," I shrugged, then grinned as inspiration came to me. "'I feel a slight stiffness coming on'?"

Brendan grimaced. "That was George Lazenby, who is nobody's favorite Bond. And I'm not actually the character I play, you know."

"Don't I know it. You've got better taste in porn, for a start."

He played with his glass a bit. "So, you like that sort of thing?"

I raised an eyebrow. "Well, I'd prefer to get to know the

bloke a bit first. Say, over dinner and a bottle of wine, that kind of thing."

Brendan drained his glass. "Dinner's over." He picked up the bottle. "And this seems to be empty," he said, and our eyes met.

I was 'round that bloody table in nought point six seconds flat.

Part of me was still thinking—and all right, there might have been a touch of hysteria in there—*oh my God, this is James Bond whose lap you just climbed onto.* The rest of me was very sensibly telling it to shut the fuck up and enjoy itself. Brendan was all lean, hard muscle—nice to know they didn't do everything with CGI. He grabbed my arse as I straddled him and pulled me closer so our dicks were pressing together through our clothes.

Clothes. That was the key word, there. As in, Get them off now before I go crazy. I pulled at Brendan's shirt and he took the hint, undoing the top two buttons then pulling it over his head. "Nice pecs," I said, a bit muffled as I had a mouthful of nipple already.

"Sort of goes with the trade," he said modestly, his breath hitching on the last word as I used my teeth. "Any—*ah*—any particular physical characteristics of the plumber I should watch out for?"

"Well, you do get a wicked strong hand grip," I told him with a grin. "Want a demonstration?"

"Of course. One can't just take these things on hearsay."

I put on the world's worst imitation of a posh accent. "Can one not, indeed?"

"Tosser," he threw back in perfect South London.

I laughed, and stripped off my T-shirt.

"Nice," Brendan said, running a hand through the hair on my chest. "I like the natural look."

"What the hell are you doing in films, then?"

"God knows. I keep thinking someone's going to pinch me and I'll wake up, Brendan Finn, jobbing actor with a great career in the catering industry to look forward to."

"I could pinch you if you like," I suggested, grabbing a nipple between thumb and forefinger and giving it a playful twist.

Brendan drew in a sharp breath. "I can think of better things you could be doing with that plumber's grip of yours."

I let my hands slide slowly down that smooth, perfect chest to his waistband. I was planning to go for slow and seductive as I undid his belt, but my fingers didn't get the message—in fact, they were aiming for the world speed record. His belt was soft, supple leather, and it slid through its loops like it'd been greased.

"Do I assume you've got plans for that?" Brendan asked, his voice low and throaty, as I snapped the leather in my hands.

"Oh, yes." He didn't resist as I stood up and pulled his hands behind the back of his chair, tying his wrists loosely together. God, he looked good, his bare chest heaving and the muscles in his shoulders standing out. Needing him so bad it hurt, I rubbed my hard-on through my jeans.

"If you're planning to reenact that scene in *Casino Royale*, I should warn you I don't do cock-and-ball torture until at least the second date," Brendan said hoarsely.

"Well, I've been round your house twice, so technically you could say this is our third date...." I winked to reassure him, and sank down to my knees on the floor between his legs. "I really hope that's not a gun in your pocket," I said, unzipping his fly. My breath caught as his cock sprang free. Long and thick, it looked like it could save the world all by itself if need be. "Fuck, that's beautiful. Have you got a license to use that thing?"

He grinned. "007, remember?"

"Going to kill me with it, are you? At least I'll die happy." I wrapped my hand around that gorgeous cock. "That grip hard enough for you?"

"God, yes," Brendan muttered, thrusting up into my hand.

"Nah, it's no good. It's still leaking," I said with mock regret and absolute truth. "Have to see if I can come up with something else to fix that." I licked my lips, then plunged my mouth down over his hard-on, taking him in deep then drawing back to tongue the tip of him. He had a rich, salty flavor that made the ache in my cock almost unbearable, so I undid my jeans and took myself in hand.

Brendan groaned. "Think...I'm...the one who's going to die happy."

Not if you kill me first, I thought, but I've got far more class than to talk with my mouth full. I pulled off him with a pop and licked all along the length of his shaft, stopping at that sensitive little spot just under the crown. Brendan bucked up in his chair, muscles straining beautifully. I gave him teasing little touches with my tongue, never quite enough. "God!" he panted. "I thought I said...no torture!"

Talking of which, I was getting a bit desperate myself. Time to put him out of my misery. I plunged my head back down and swallowed round him, right hand playing with his balls while the left pumped up and down like a piston on my hard-on. Brendan gave a strangled groan as he shot his load down my throat, and I made a right pig's ear of his expensive trousers with my jizz a moment later.

After I'd stopped shuddering, I rested my head on his knee for a moment, then I got up a bit shakily and untied his hands. "Sorry about the mess."

Brendan looked at his legs. "That's actually quite impressive. Have you been saving yourself for me?"

I grinned. "Nah, just wanted to give you an excuse to stay the night. We can bung those in the wash, they'll be dry by morning. Unless you've got somewhere to dash off to? Worlds to save, women to screw? Or maybe just premieres to attend?" I didn't cross my fingers. I just thought hopeful thoughts.

Brendan pulled me in close for a kiss. It was slow and thorough, tasting of wine, garlic, and a kind of surprised happiness. "There's no hurry. At the risk of tempting fate rather badly— we've got all the time in the world."

I leaned back and gave him a look. "Now who's quoting George Lazenby?"

"Touché. Well, if a bald man in a neck brace should happen along, just make sure you remember to duck."

"Too right. If anyone shoots me in the head before I can get you into bed and implement stage two of the evil master plan, I'm going to be well peeved."

Brendan raised an eyebrow. "Evil master plan? Does that involve world domination?"

"Well, maybe not the world," I told him with a wicked smile. "But I reckon I could manage the domination, if you're up for it."

He grinned, those gray-blue eyes glittering like sapphires in the sun. "Just give me ten minutes. Then I'll definitely be up for it."

THE VIRGIN PRINCE AND THE REBEL CHIEF

Red Morgan

P rince Tomas watched as, in a far-off valley, a light appeared. Three more followed. "I see the rebels are little braver tonight," King Olaf said as he joined his son on the palace balcony. "We will teach them a lesson they won't forget for a long time."

"But Father, I have heard they defend the poor and weak and that they only..."

"I'll hear no more of that talk, my boy. They are nothing but a bunch of vagabonds and thieves. I will post more guards. Nothing must interfere with the Midsummer Ball." King Olaf clasped his son's shoulder. "Your mother has invited the most beautiful girls from near and far. Tomorrow, we will find you a bride."

Tomas moved away, watching the distant flames flicker and dance in the still, dark night. "Father, is it wrong to want someone to love, someone who takes your breath away just at the sight of them?"

"No, son, and tomorrow one of those beauties just might do that."

Tomas shook his head and glanced nervously at his father. It was now or never. "I don't think I'll find that person tomorrow at the ball."

"Not even Lady Angelina? She's a renowned beauty, clever and a gifted healer, like your mother."

"No, not even the beautiful Angelina."

"A marriage between you two would make a strong alliance."

"She hasn't got what I'm looking for in a soul mate."

"And what is that, my boy?"

Tomas sighed and waited for his father's look of disappointment. "A cock."

There was only understanding on the king's face. "I wondered when you would admit it, to me and to yourself."

"You know I like men?"

King Olaf nodded.

"How do you know?"

"I've seen your hungry eyes for the tight, encased bottoms and bare, muscled chests of the stable boys. And ..." The king paused. "I know because I felt like you at your age."

Trying to hide the look of shock, Tomas turned to face his father. "But you married Mother?"

"It has been a good marriage, and make no mistake, I love her dearly. It's worked because we both wanted the alliance, we both wanted a child, and we both maintained our own interests. As you know, your mother likes dancing, shopping, and herbal lore and I like hunting and young, willing men."

"I can't marry a woman just to make a good alliance."

"Times have changed. We'll arrange another ball, this time with the most handsome men in the realm."

Tomas's face lit up at the thought of all that muscle and cock and then the smile disappeared. "But Father, I won't marry for anything less than love."

"We shall see Tomas, we shall see."

The next day, the prince walked into the stable. The twins, Daniel and David, were brushing down the royal steeds. Both boys wore ragged, holey short breeches in the early morning heat, showing more than a glimpse of muscular thigh. Their bare chests glistened with manly sweat though they were barely seventeen. Both boys turned around at the prince's entrance.

"Sire, can we help you?"

Tomas licked his lips, watching as a rivulet of perspiration ran down David's tanned chest. For a moment their eyes held and Tomas began to feel the familiar sensation of arousal. He craved it, but he was scared of it, in equal measure. He was untouched by male or female, and even now at nineteen, the thought of true intimacy frightened him.

"I shall take Bessie out for a run this morning." He attached the bag of healing herbs and salve he always carried with him to the horse's saddle.

David walked up to the prince's side. "Sire, you are so tense. Let me massage your shoulders, else Bessie will pick up on your tension and be skittish."

The groom began kneading the tight knots. "You are so stiff. Let me work all that tension out of you." The young boy's breath was warm on Tomas's neck.

Tomas could feel his cock growing. He could feel the tension moving from his shoulders to a different part of his body. If he didn't get away he was going to cum in his breeches. "That's enough, David, thank you."

"I am your servant, Sire. You have only to ask and I will be at your bidding."

Tomas mounted his horse and rode out of the stables without another word. Five minutes away he let go of the reins and let the horse wander. He was still semi-aroused from his encounter with the groom so he let his thoughts linger on the image of being touched for the first time by a man. How their naked bodies would glide together. Reaching down, Tomas gave his hardening shaft a light stroke to encourage the thrill of arousal to linger.

What Tomas wanted was a man, but not just any man. He wanted one who was tall and strong and a little bit domineering. Often he would watch the knights practicing their sword play and imagine Sir Niall's hot body on top of him. He would dash off to his room and rub his cock till it spurted.

Tomas reached down again. He was as hard as iron. It wouldn't take him long to spill his seed. Thoughts of Niall taking him roughly from behind, and a few strong strokes of his hand, would be enough. He looked around and spotted a small coppice to his left. Tying his mount to a nearby branch, he fished out his straining erection. It felt hot and needy. Wrapping his fist around the solid flesh, he murmured with pleasure at the first stroke.

A few feet away a twig snapped. Before he had time to put his stiff prick away, Tomas was surrounded by five beefy, brawny men, all dressed in leather trousers and waistcoats, showing their bare torsos off to good advantage.

The oldest of the men, obviously the leader, said, "Well, well, what have we got ourselves here, a right little plaything to keep us happy for the next few nights? Look he's got his cock out ready for us."

Tomas daren't move and willed his erection to go down, but it stubbornly refused. Even though he was scared he was aroused by the men's bodies.

"Hold his arms while I suck on his cock." The leader said, rubbing his hands together with evident glee.

Tomas's cock twitched in response at the thought that at least he was going to feel a pair of lips engulfing his frustrated prick. At the same time he was disappointed that the first person to touch him wasn't someone he could fall in love with.

Just as the man fell to his knees, another grabbed Tomas's chin. "Wait, Gawain, isn't this Prince Tomas, the king's only child?"

Gawain looked up. "Are you?"

Tomas glanced down and surveyed the full, moist lips of his captor and decided he could wait for love. What he wanted was that heavenly mouth bringing him to completion.

"Do what you will with me, I'll tell you nothing."

Gawain grabbed Tomas's chin. "Tell me, are you the prince?"

Tomas stayed resolutely silent.

Another of the men said, "If he is, the chief will want him unharmed and untouched."

Gawain looked disappointed. "You are right, that way we'll get a good ransom for him. Tie his hands behind his back." Gawain stepped forward and palmed Tomas's cock, giving it a slow, deliberate rub with his thumb. "Best get everything put away and you looking decent before you meet the chief. And mark my words, if you're not the prince then you are mine." He turned to one of the men and said, "Put him on his horse and blindfold him so he doesn't know the way to our camp."

As they rode along at a steady pace Tomas tried to keep from shaking so much that he fell off the horse. He'd heard many rumors, none of them good, about the rebel band of cutthroats. After about an hour of travelling they came to a halt. Someone grabbed him and pulled him off the horse, throwing him to the floor. Tomas could hear voices all around him.

"Go tell the chief about our guest and ask him what he wants us to do."

A minute later, one of the men called out. "The chief wants him in his tent. He says keep him tied and blindfolded."

Tomas was pulled to his feet and then pushed in the direction of his fate. As he entered the tent, he heard, "So this is our guest. Handsome fellow."

The voice was like warm, melted chocolate. Tomas was pleased that he was blindfolded so he could concentrate on the voice that sent shivers up and down his spine. And his back wasn't the only part of his body it was affecting.

Tomas tensed as he felt hot breath on his neck. "I'm not the prince, if that is what you are going to ask me."

"No, that wasn't what I was going to ask." The warm air on his neck and the sensual voice in his ear made Tomas's legs weak with desire. "I already know you are Prince Tomas. I want to know what plans your father has to put an end to my band of rebels."

"I'm telling you nothing."

Tomas felt cold metal pressed against his throat. He swallowed convulsively, aware that this could be either his last day on earth or a moment's deferment before the torture started. The knife slid down the front of his tunic, slicing through the material and leaving his chest bare. A finger rubbed his nipple, at first gentle and then harder, ending in a painful but pleasurable squeeze, causing him to yelp. Hot lips sucked on his neck. He stood still, not daring to move as the chief walked around to stand at the back of him. Tomas could feel the hard muscles of the broad chest pressed up against his back. Further down he could feel a hard cock rubbing against his nervous ass.

"Do you have anything to tell me?" A tongue licked at his ear. Tomas was frightened, aroused, and, most of all, confused.

It was more like a seduction than an interrogation.

He took a deep breath, trying to steady his voice as nerves twisted his bowels in fear. "Sir, and I only call you Sir because I do not know your name. I imagined that my first time would be with a man I loved. I just ask that when you rape me you remember I am not an animal."

"You're a virgin?"

Not trusting his voice, Tomas replied with a nod.

Sensual lips toyed with his neck. "The gods shine on me today. My own little virgin prince."

Tomas gasped as a hand reached around and rubbed his cock to life. "I don't intend to rape you, Prince Tomas. When I finally make love to you, it will be after you have begged me to."

"That hardly seems likely. I suspect if I don't you will take me anyway?"

The hand squeezed and Tomas could feel himself growing unbearably aroused. "You will beg," the voice whispered before the hands and lips disappeared.

The chief moved away from Thomas. "Gawain, take our guest to the main tent, feed him, take him to the latrines, let him clean up. Return him to me, tied and blindfolded."

"Aye, Chief."

No one spoke to Tomas as he sat at the campfire eating rabbit stew and fresh baked bread, but the people around him seemed happy enough. They weren't the savages and ruffians his father had made them out to be. They were clean and civilized. They played music and danced. Gawain came and sat down by him, with his own bowl of stew and chunk of bread.

"What do you make of our camp and our people?"

"Truthfully, it's not like I imagined. You have families here and sick people."

"Where else are they to go?"

"They could ask for help from the king."

"Yes, of course they could."

"Why can't I keep my blindfold off?"

"The chief wants you to wear it when you are with him."

"Why?"

The rebel shrugged. "He has his ways. We don't question them." Gawain stood and pulled Tomas to his feet. "Come on, let's get you ready for a good night's sleep."

Tomas was tied and blindfolded and led back to the chief's tent and thrown to the floor.

The chief leaned over him. "Settle down and sleep. I have an early start in the morning." The voice was gruff and weary, the smooth, seductive tones gone.

As Thomas struggled to fall asleep, listening to the chief's soft snoring, he tried to put out of his mind the feeling of an experienced hand on his cock. He knew sleep would be a long way off.

The next morning, he awoke to Gawain's gentle kick to his side. "Get up, it's time for something to eat." His blindfold was taken off as he walked out into a dull, gray morning. "Get some breakfast, go to the latrine and then we'll find you something to do."

"Where's the chief?"

Instead of answering him, Gawain said, "Cedric, when his highness here has finished washing and having a morning piss, tie his leg to one of the stakes so he can't run off and set him to skinning some rabbits."

Tomas paled. "I've never skinned a rabbit."

A sneer came over the man's face. "No, I don't suppose you've done a day's hard work in your little, privileged life."

Tomas held his chin high, even though he felt like curling up into a ball and crying. "No, I don't suppose I have."

"Set him chopping the vegetables. Even he should be capable of chopping carrots without getting into any mischief."

As Tomas began cutting the vegetables he got talking to one of the women skinning the rabbits. "Is the chief a good man?"

"Don't you believe what you've heard about him. He looks after the sick, the poor, and the ones who've been ill treated by those who should know better."

"Where is he now?"

"Gone scouting and poaching. It's not easy to feed this many people."

Hours later, when Tomas felt like his fingers were going to drop off and his back would break, he heard the sounds of horses crashing through the forest as the hunting party returned.

Tomas tried to deny to himself the feeling of excitement that rushed through his body at the thought of the chief's return and his first glance at his face. He hoped that it was handsome and strong, to match the voice and the gentle hands and not marked by scars or signs of pox. Before he got chance to find out, someone approached from behind and replaced the blindfold.

Later, as he ate his food shackled and blind, Tomas could hear the chief's dulcet tones regaling stories of the day's hunting. Abruptly he was pulled to his feet.

"Torture time." The chief's velvet voice said in his ear.

As they entered the tent, Tomas stood rigid with fear. He was stripped naked and fastened to a pole in the middle of the tent.

"Tell me what your father has planned."

Tomas stayed silent.

There was a nip on his neck and a hand slipped to his groin. "Tell me what you know."

Tomas couldn't follow the lines of questioning as a firm hand took hold of his cock. He felt a light kiss on the tip of his hardening shaft. He had been expecting pain and instead he was experiencing pleasure. A wet, warm tongue made its way up the full length of his erection. He waited for the mouth to enclose him, to take him in and suck him to heaven. The lips retreated and he felt a tongue on his heavy balls. He arched, wanting more.

"You're not far from completion. Tell me what your father has planned and I will give you an orgasm like you've never known in your life."

"I can't tell you."

Tomas screamed out as a bucket of ice cold water was thrown on his groin. As he was released from the pole, he curled up, cold, wet, and miserable. The chief didn't say another word.

The next morning, Tomas peeled vegetables again. This time, the chief and his band did not return before the evening meal, and he was placed in the chief's tent alone. As he was drifting off to sleep he heard footsteps outside.

"I hope you are not asleep, my little captive." Tomas's body responded to the honeyed tones. "Stand." Tomas obeyed. The rope around his wrists was untied.

"Just in case you get the wrong idea, I have a dagger ready, so do as I say and don't make any foolish moves. Understand?"

Tomas nodded.

"Take your clothes off."

"All of them?"

"Yes, slowly."

Tomas slipped off his torn tunic. "I thought you said you wouldn't rape me."

"Take off your breeches. Stretch out your hands." His hands were retied. "Lay down on the floor."

Tomas lay on his belly.

"Turn over, onto your back."

As he lay in the dark, Tomas trembled with fear and anticipation. His body jerked as a tongue toyed with the tip of his cock, tickling and teasing him to full arousal.

"You like that, don't you, Tomas? Do you want me to suck you?"

"I'm not going to tell you anything and I'm not going to beg."

"I didn't ask that. I asked if you wanted me to take you in my mouth."

The prince gave a discernable nod before turning his head away, ashamed of his need. His prick was engulfed by a warm, wet mouth, but only for a moment. He felt the weight of the other man, now naked, press down on him, their erections rubbing together.

"You are a very desirable man, my virgin prince, very desirable indeed."

Tomas felt lightheaded as lips played on his sensitive neck.

"I want you. My lips want you, my body wants you, most of all, my hard cock wants you."

Tomas thrust up, wanting more pressure. "I'm not going to beg." His voice was weak.

"We'll see."

The weight lifted off him but the sensation was quickly replaced by sensuous lips sucking at his nipple. The chief's hand expertly brought him near to climax. Just as Tomas was getting used to the rhythm of the hand it was replaced by a talented mouth, and the hands began an exploration of his body. He could feel the explosion of need building, coalescing in his innards, ready to blow. The mouth retreated.

"What is your father planning?"

Tomas groaned in frustration and brought his hands down, trying to bring himself to climax. His hands were pushed away.

"So near, Tomas, so near."

Icy water rained down on him.

The next morning, like the day before, the chief was gone when Tomas woke up.

After the evening meal, he was bathed, stripped, naked, blindfolded, and tied to the stake, a wolf skin thrown over him. His nakedness made him nervous. The chief had still not returned. A breeze blew across his exposed back as someone entered the tent.

"Ah my little virgin prince, I see they've prepared you for my return."

"I'm not your plaything. I intend to fight every inch of the way!"

The chief took in a deep breath. "I'd be disappointed if you didn't, but first I must eat. I'll be back."

Tomas closed his eyes in disappointment and was half-dozing when he felt the wolf skin pulled off him.

"You have beautiful lips." The chief kissed Tomas's pink, soft mouth. The tongue traced the shape of the full lips, teasing them open before plunging in. "You have a well-developed chest for someone who's never known hard work and nipples that tease me." A tongue played with the swollen buds and the sharp teeth gave a gentle nip. Tomas tried to think of terrible things to persuade his cock from responding. A hand caressed his pale inner thigh. Tomas shivered.

"You have strong legs and I find the thought of those legs around my waist very arousing." A tongue trailed all the way from Tomas's knee to his groin. "Does the thought of you holding me tight within your strong thighs arouse you, little prince? You don't have to answer. I see that it does."

A finger travelled from the root to the tip of Tomas's rock-hard shaft.

"And now we get to the best." A tongue swirled around the

head. "Your cock is the most delicious I've seen in a long time. A perfect shape. I want to lick it." The talented tongue left a warm, wet trail. "I want to suckle it." The wet mouth sucked the end. "And I want to gobble it all up." Tomas gasped as his cock slid into the welcome cavern. He bit down on his lips, hard enough to draw blood, just so he wouldn't beg to be fucked and fucked hard.

The mouth, as the night before, was taken away but the lips moved to his neck. "See how aroused you make me, Tomas, how hard I am for you." Tomas's hand was placed on the chief's erection. "Does it feel good, can you imagine it sliding into you, giving you pleasure? Can you imagine it, more pleasure than you have ever known?"

"Yes, I can imagine it," Tomas replied, his voice hoarse with arousal.

The chief moved away for a second, and Tomas was going to call out when a mouth surrounded his cock. This time it was joined by a blunt, oiled finger circling his tight sphincter.

Tomas wanted more of the mouth, wanted the finger to breach his virgin hole, wanted to climax more than anything."

"Do you want to cum, Tomas?"

"Yes." He half-groaned and half-sobbed.

"Tell me, what are your father's plans?"

The mouth deep-throated him, the finger pressed a little harder.

"One of your rebels has been captured. He's to be hanged at the fair at Wood Bottom on Lady's Day. When you attempt to rescue the condemned man, as my father knows you will, your gang will be ambushed and brought to justice."

"We will be in disguise. How will he know us among the crowd?"

"You have a traitor in your camp. He will point you out."

"Do you know this bastard's name?"

"I can't tell you."

The finger and mouth retreated. "Do you want to cum?"

"Yes."

"Tell me."

"Caleb Swiftfoot."

"Good, and now you get your reward." The mouth went to work on the frustrated prick and the finger teased its way into the tight tunnel.

The waves of pleasure ripping through his body sent Tomas into spasm after spasm. Never in all his nineteen years had he felt such bliss. He was exhausted. He was in heaven. He was in love. The chief lay down beside him. "Touch me." He guided Tomas's hand to his hard prick. "Make me cum."

Afterward, Tomas was surprised when he was pulled into muscular arms. "Tonight we sleep together." Tomas was even more surprised at the tender kiss. "One day, before we release you, I hope I hear you beg for me to make love to you."

"I won't beg."

Tomas was surprised when he awoke still in the rebel's arm. "Let me take off the blindfold, let me see your face."

"You can see my face when I make love to you. Think on that. I have to go now, and let's hope the information you have given me is correct."

"You're going to fight them?"

"That would be foolish; we are greatly outnumbered."

"So what are you going to do?"

"Not lie down and take it like a doxy, that's for sure."

It was a long day for Tomas as he was taught to skin rabbits and clear out the pig pen. As the stew was nearly ready, there were shouts for help coming from the trees. Out into the clearing Gawain led a team carrying a man laid on a makeshift stretcher.

"Get the healer," he shouted.

An old woman stepped forward. "He's over at Clovehampton, there's been an outbreak of the fever and some of the children need medication."

Tomas stood and joined the crowd gathered around the injured man. "I'm a healer. Let me take a look at him."

Gawain shook his head. "How would you know about healing, little prince?"

"Because my mother is a renowned healer and she taught me."

"'Tis true, I worked at the castle in my youth and I heard of the queen performing miracles," the woman said.

Gawain thought for a moment. He turned to the men who had carried the stretcher. "Take him to his tent." He turned to Tomas. "If he dies at your hands, then you will die at mine."

Tomas ignored him. "I need hot water, clean cloth to make bandages and have you got the bag I had when I was captured?"

"Yes, somewhere."

"It contains salve and a healing draught. Find it." Tomas watched as the injured man was ferried to the chief's hut.

As the men placed the stretcher on the floor and turned to leave, Tomas stopped Gawain. "Do you normally bring the injured to the chief's hut?"

"We do when he's the chief."

Tomas's heart speeded up. For a moment he forgot about the injuries as he took his first look at the man who had not only captured him but had captured his heart. Tomas looked over the powerfully built arms and strong hands; they could kill someone or they could protect someone. He liked the idea of being protected by the chief. The leather tunic accentuated the smooth, broad chest, clear of any hair. Wrapped in those arms, pressed against that body, Tomas knew he would be in heaven.

One of the men sat in the corner with crossed legs. "Orders from Gawain so you're not tempted to hasten the chief to his death."

A woman came in with a bowl of water, some clean rags, and his bag. Tomas kneeled down. He allowed himself a moment to look at his jailor's face. It was a strong face, handsome in a rugged way. The dark hair, damp with sweat, stuck to his brow and lay in loose curls around his shoulders. Snapping out of his enjoyment at looking at the unconscious man, he pulled the tunic away from the wound. The blood started flowing again and Tomas pressed a pad of material to stem the flow. Working quickly, Tomas cleaned up the wound, realizing that it looked worse than it actually was. Smothering on the salve, Tomas began to bind the gash as best he could. As he tried to lift up the dead weight of the injured man, the chief's eyes flickered open.

"I'm sorry, I know you are in pain, but if you could just sit up a little, I can do a better job with the dressing." Tomas turned to the man in the corner. "Help, we need to get this done quickly."

A tortured groan echoed through the tent as they struggled with the binding. Tomas let out a sigh of relief as the chief fell back into a deep sleep.

That night Tomas slept outside with the others. The next morning, he was allowed back in to tend the dressing. As he finished, the chief's eyes opened, and he said, "Thank you."

"Drink this draught. It will ease the pain."

By lunchtime, Tomas had managed to find out what had happened. The last of the rebels had returned home, a few more with injuries. As it was the day before the fair, they had managed to get the prisoner free without any trouble, taking the jailer by surprise. It was as they'd made their way from the village that they had run into a scouting party. The fighting had been vicious, but there had been no fatalities on either side. As he finished attending the last of the injured, Gawain walked over to him. "Come with me. The chief is asking for you."

Tomas was pleased to see some color in the chief's cheeks. "How are you feeling?"

"Thanks to you, much better than I should, considering the damage I took. I'll be back on my horse by tomorrow."

"No you won't. You're still weak."

"Are you giving me orders, my own handsome prince?"

Tomas blushed. "You're not to get on a horse. The wound will start to bleed again."

The chief gave a wan smile. "Gawain, leave us alone."

"Is that wise?"

"He didn't save me to then plunge a knife in me."

When they were alone, the chief turned to Tomas. "You are free to go."

"What?" Tomas didn't mean to sound disappointed but he expected something more dramatic than this. "But I haven't begged yet and you said..."

"You are free to go. My men will blindfold you and see you far away from here. I ask just one last kiss good-bye."

The prince knelt down and placed a tender kiss on the chief's mouth. He reached up and stroked his cheek. "But I still don't know what it's like to feel a man inside me."

The chief placed a hand over the prince's. "You don't know how you tempted me in the night, with your pale body beckoning me in the firelight. Go before I weaken."

"I won't go, not until you've made love to me."

The prince pulled off his tunic and kicked off his breeches, joining the injured man under the fur skin.

"I want to take you, here and now, but you are a good man and deserve someone better, someone you can love."

"Maybe I've already found him." Tomas placed a trail of kisses down the chief's neck ending with a deep kiss on the lips. Breaking away, Tomas kissed his way down the broad expanse of chest and smiled to see that the wound hadn't affected the chief's ardor. He wasn't sure what to do next, but he remembered what he liked so he began licking his way up the hard cock. "You're too weak to make love so we'll have to make do with this."

"Don't be too sure about that." The chief rolled Tomas over onto his back, pinning him to the floor. "Just be gentle with me. But first I want you to beg."

"I told you, I'm not begging."

"So you're telling me, you don't want my cock inside you, thrusting in and out, bringing you wave after wave of pleasure?"

"Yes I want it. I want you."

"You want me to fuck you."

They both groaned as their erections rubbed together.

"Yes, make love to me. Please. Take me. Now."

The kisses trailing down Tomas's neck were slow, sensual, and seductive. "You will be gentle with me, won't you?" Tomas said, arching up to allow full contact between their erections.

Groaning, the chief rolled off the prince onto his side. "I think I'll need to be gentle for both of us."

Tomas sat up, his face full of concern. "I told you. What you need to…"

"What I need is you. What I need is to kiss you, to touch you." The chief's finger left a soft trail from the pale, freckled shoulder to the tip of the index finger. Tomas shuddered.

"What I need is to be in you." Pulling Tomas closer to him, he kissed the full mouth with increasing hunger. "I'm going to make love to you, just not as energetically as I'd have liked. Turn onto your side, away from me."

Tomas did as instructed, nestling up against the brawny chest. He murmured his approval as he felt a soft nip at his earlobe. Tomas's cock began to harden as a hand stroked down his chest, toying with a nipple before caressing his flat belly. He closed his eyes, wanting desperately for the hand to touch him in a more intimate place. Instead, the hand softly stroked up his inner thigh. Tomas's cock jerked in appreciation.

"Hmm, that feels so good." Tomas moaned, his hand reaching around to pull the chief's head closer. Kisses and bites worked their way down his neck as a finger played through his curly pubic hair.

"Please!" Tomas begged.

"What do you want me to do?"

"Touch me."

Tomas could hear the smile in his lover's voice. "Not yet."

A hand cupped and kneaded his taut ass cheek, a small finger teasing his ass.

"Please."

The chief sucked hard on Tomas's neck as his hand moved back around to the front, cupping the full orbs, toying with them.

Tomas grabbed the hand, placing it on the rock hard shaft.

"Stroke it, please."

"Let's get one thing straight, I'm in charge and I'm in no rush." The chief's breath was warm in Tomas's ear.

The chief reached for something and Tomas felt an oiled finger stroke down his ass crack, playing with his hole. "Do you want my finger inside you?"

Tomas craved to be touched in the most intimate parts of his body, he craved to be filled, to explode with desire. Tomas nodded.

The finger rubbed over the puckered entrance and then with-drew. Before Tomas had time to give a groan of disappointment, a hand wrapped around his distressed cock. An oily stroke started the journey to orgasmic bliss.

"Oh, God, yes." After so much teasing, Tomas felt so close to cumming. "Oh, God." The feelings were building. He wanted to hold them back, he wanted to make the feelings last. But more, he wanted release. He reached around and grabbed the chief's hair, relishing every kiss on his neck and shoulders. "Oh." The hand was gone. "No. Please. More."

"Who did I say was in charge?"

"You."

"And I say, not yet."

A slick finger slipped through the ring of resistance and Tomas called out, more in surprise and pleasure than discom-fort. "More."

Fingers filled him, stretched him, gave him sensations he'd never experienced before, and then they were gone and something thicker, harder and more terrifying was trying to enter him.

"Do you want me?" The chief's husky voice broke into Tomas's lust-addled mind.

"More than anything."

The chief's cock pushed in a little further. Tomas gasped. He was scared he wouldn't be able to take any more.

"And I want you more than anyone I've ever had before."

Tomas's ass was breached a little further. "We're nearly there. But I want to know one thing before you get all of my hard, needy desire."

Tomas could hardly think now the chief's hand had moved back onto his neglected shaft. "What do you want to know?" Tomas managed to ask, his concentration on the hard cock up his ass and the firm hand on his shaft.

"Do you love me?"

"Oh." Tomas bit his lip as the well-oiled cock began to move in and out. "Oh definitely." His dick was being stroked by a warm, experienced hand. "Yes, I love you. Oh, I love…I…" A cum-soaked explosion took Tomas's breath away. He pushed his body back to meet the chief's last thrust.

As Tomas lay in post-orgasmic bliss, muscular arms keeping him warm and safe, he thought about his future. The only one he could come up with was one with the chief. Would it be the life of an outlaw? Or would his father see sense and talk to the rebels so they could all live in peace? He reached out and stroked the rugged face. "You've captured me, you've tortured me, though in a very enjoyable way, and you've made love to me and I still don't know your name."

"My name is Adam but when we're making love, you can call me Chief if that's what you like." He laughed and showed a wonderful smile.

"No, I like Adam, my first man."

The chief leant over, placing a kiss on his forehead. "Your only man, I hope."

THE PRINCE OF EISENGRAF

Neil Plakcy

Don't be silly, Rhys," Elaina said. "A boy can't fall in love with a handsome prince and live happily ever after."

Elaina and I were both seven years old, next-door neighbors. We had just finished watching a tape of Disney's *Cinderella* for about the fifteenth time, and I had announced what I knew my future held.

I can still see that scene. Elaina went to Catholic school, and that afternoon she was still wearing her school clothes, a white blouse and plaid skirt, though she'd tossed aside her patent leather Mary Janes when we settled on the couch in her den.

I wore my favorite pink polo shirt and blue jeans. Elaina's mother had made us a big bowl of microwave popcorn, and by the end of the movie all that were left were the unpopped kernels.

"I'm going to meet a handsome prince," she said. "My mother says there's a prince for every little girl."

I started to argue but gave up. When Elaina got mad at me,

she wouldn't let me come over and play tea party with her or watch videos. But I was determined that I was going to meet and fall in love with my own handsome prince.

I wish I could go back to my seven-year-old self and talk to that little blond boy, the one who walked on his tippy-toes like a ballerina, who played with his sister's Barbies when she wasn't there, who knew even then where his affections would lie. What would I tell him? That Elaina was wrong—a boy can fall in love with a handsome prince. But the happily ever after part? That's still up in the air.

By the time I was thirty, I'd given up on my seven-year-old fantasy. No handsome prince was going to sweep in and remove me from my failure of a life. I had finished a master's degree in folklore from the University of Oregon, which qualified me for nothing. My only significant emotional relationship had turned out to be a farce, and I'd abandoned my friends and family to move across the country, landing in Miami Beach, where good gay boys can get a fabulous tan. Elaina and I were still friends, though our relationship was confined to Facebook. She was a good Catholic girl who couldn't have sex until she was married, so she did so right after high school.

I was an adjunct instructor at the community college, teaching Introduction to Folklore, which paid me just enough to cover the rent. In order to eat, I took a second job, working at a bookstore on Lincoln Road, the pedestrian thoroughfare where everyone goes to see and be seen and sometimes to shop.

Things were slow on Thursdays, and that afternoon I was the only staffer in the store. There was just one customer, a trim, handsome man about my age. I was going back and forth between the counter and the storeroom, packing up books for an author event at a senior citizens' condo while the guy browsed.

I couldn't help stealing a few glances at him. His tailored slacks and button-down shirt screamed money, and he wore a thick gold bracelet and a gold signet ring. His polished black loafers looked like Ferragamos. His black hair had been expertly cut, and his goatee and mustache gave him a saturnine look.

When I had all the books packed up, I walked over to where he stood. "Can I help you find anything?"

I noticed he was carrying a copy of John Morgan Wilson's latest Benjamin Justice mystery. "If you like Wilson, we have a number of other detective books. Anthony Bidulka writes a private eye series out of Saskatchewan. Josh Lanyon's books are about a bookseller in Pasadena, and Neil Plakcy's are about a police detective in Honolulu."

"Well," he said. "I do need some more to read."

His Eastern European accent, overlaid with British inflections, sent pleasant shivers down my spine. I led him down the stack, picking out one book from each author and handing them to him.

While he scanned the jackets, I tidied up a couple of shelves of Florida mysteries. He looked up from the last book, the ends of his mouth pointed down. "These are all gay detectives," he said.

"Well, yes," I said. "I thought that's what you were looking for."

He blushed.

"Sorry. I didn't mean to assume." I reached for the books, but he held on to them.

"This may be quite forward of me," he said. "But perhaps I could convince you to have dinner with me? We could talk about books."

He didn't want to meet my eyes. *Well, well,* I thought. "That would be nice. There are a bunch of great little places here on Lincoln Road." I looked at my watch. It was almost five. "My replacement should be here in about ten or fifteen minutes," I said. "If you wanted to go then?"

He lifted his head and met my gaze, and his blue-gray eyes sent sensations of a whole other kind to my groin. I didn't usually eat out; my budget only extended to pasta, soup, and the occasional $5 submarine sandwich. But I'd eat rice and beans for a month for the chance to share a meal with this gorgeous hunk with the sexy accent.

"I should pay you for these," he said.

I walked over to the register and started ringing them up. "Oh," he said, opening his wallet. "I don't have as much cash as I thought."

"That's fine. We take credit cards."

He hesitated, and the first thing that came to my mind was "closeted."

"There won't be anything on the bill that says what you bought," I said. "Just the name of the store."

The tension in his body relieved a bit, and he smiled. He handed me his card, which I swiped through the authorization gizmo. "Wolfgang von Eisengraf," I said, looking at the name on the card. "Like the country."

"Just Wolf. You know Eisengraf?"

I nodded, as I handed him the card and the charge slip to sign. "I used to have a fascination for those forgotten principalities and grand duchies of Europe," I said. "I wrote my master's thesis on the crossover of folklore traditions from the larger countries, like France and Germany, to the smaller ones, like Monaco, Luxembourg, and Eisengraf."

He signed the slip and handed it back to me, and I felt stupid. I didn't reveal any of my personal background to customers; to most of them, I was just a clerk there to provide recommendations and ring up purchases.

My replacement came in a few minutes later, and Wolf and I walked out to Lincoln Road. "I don't even know your name," he said, as we walked out to the street.

"I'm sorry," I said. "I'm Rhys. Rhys Jones."

"A solid Welsh name." We shook hands, as if we'd just met. "Are you Welsh?"

"My father was," I said. "He died when I was five. I started reading Welsh fairy tales then, to try and connect with him, I guess."

"And that led you to study folklore?"

"Yes, I guess it did," I said, though I hadn't made the connection until then. My mom raised me as a single parent, never remarrying, and I'd spent my childhood with my nose in books. I'd gone on from Welsh folklore to the Brothers Grimm and Hans Christian Andersen. In my teens I'd read a lot of adult fantasy, much of it rooted in that Welsh mythology I'd started with as a child.

"Are you from Eisengraf?" I asked Wolf, as we walked down toward Collins Avenue, staying to the shady side of the street.

"You could say that," he said. "My family goes back there many generations."

I struggled to remember what I knew of Eisengraf. Germany had once been a patchwork of sovereign states. Toward the end of the nineteenth century, King Wilhelm of Prussia had brought those states together as one country and become Emperor Wilhelm I, also known as Kaiser Wilhelm.

Prince Karl of Eisengraf had declared his loyalty to Wilhelm but refused to join the alliance, choosing, like the titular heads of Lichtenstein and Luxembourg, to remain independent. I'd never been to Eisengraf, but I had studied it quite a lot, making connections between its political interdependence with Germany and the intersection of its folkloric traditions.

We stopped at a cross street to let a Rolls Royce pass, and I remembered that in Germany, since the Weimar Republic, all titles are considered part of one's last name. Wolf's last name was von Eisengraf. Did that mean he was part of the ruling family?

I was lost in thought until Wolf said, "There is a restaurant I would like to try. Joe's Stone Crab, I believe it is called. We do not get much fresh seafood at home."

I had to nip that idea in the bud. You could do some serious damage at a place like Joe's. I'd been thinking of a tiny sandwich shop a few blocks down, where I could escape for under ten bucks. "I'm afraid that's a little out of my budget."

"Of course, you are my guest for dinner," Wolf said. "I could not conceive of expecting you to pay for your meal when I invited you."

"Then Joe's it is," I said. We took a cab down to the tip of Miami Beach, and I noticed that Wolf tipped the cabbie generously.

The maitre d' took one look at Wolf, in his elegant, expertly tailored shirt and slacks, and me in my T-shirt and shorts, and spoke directly to him. But ever the gentleman, Wolf ushered me ahead of him as the maitre d' led us to a table. Or maybe he just wanted to look at my ass.

I couldn't figure him out. Was he gay? Why would he have invited me to dinner if he wasn't? Was he just lonely, a foreign businessman looking for company while he ate?

I expected him to order a bottle of fancy wine, but when the server arrived he ordered a Sea Dog raspberry wheat, and I said, "I'll have the same."

"You like beer?" he asked.

"Fruit beers and pale ales. Nothing too heavy. It's too hot for lagers or porters."

"I like a man who knows his tastes," Wolf said. "You can recommend something from the menu?"

"Sorry, this is my first time. My budget stops at fast food these days."

"In Europe, a bookseller is an honorable profession," he said. "But in America, it seems most of the staff I have seen in bookstores have not yet outgrown their acne."

I laughed. "You must have been visiting the chain bookstores."

"Yes. It is very hard to find...books of a unique character, without having to ask many staff."

"You mean gay books." I figured we'd get that word on the table right away.

"Yes, but also historical fiction, poetry—anything that is not on your best-seller lists."

The server brought our beers, and without asking decanted them into tall pilsner glasses. Then he launched into a long dissertation on the specials, along with his personal recommendations for appetizers and entrees. Wolf sat there listening as if the waiter was the most important person in the world.

I couldn't get over the prices. I'd never had a guy take me out to such an expensive restaurant before.

"Shall I order for you?" Wolf asked me.

"Sure."

He ordered us bowls of stone crab bisque, a pair of two-pound Maine lobsters broiled with spinach stuffing, and sides of hash browns and grilled tomatoes. "I have a large appetite," he said, and smiled at me, and I could only call the look on his face wolfish.

I could eat for a week on what that meal cost. I hoped for his sake that Wolf had a good-paying job back in Eisengraf.

I picked up my beer, took a sip. It was good. "You said your family has been in Eisengraf for a long time," I said. "So does that mean you're related to the prince regent?"

"Actually, I am the prince regent. Though I've only had the title for a year and I'm not quite accustomed to it yet."

I spit some beer back into the glass, nearly choking. Smooth move. "Excuse me? You're the prince regent of Eisengraf?"

"Shh. I don't like people to make a fuss."

"You'll forgive me," I said. "I'm a little shell-shocked. I've never known an actual prince before."

Wolf shrugged. "That's why I am careful who I tell. People change." He looked at me. "Will you change your attitude toward me?"

And just what was that attitude? I asked myself. I still thought he was cute, and I loved that sexy accent. "Nope. I figured we were going to talk about books, and as long as you can still read I don't see anything changing."

Wolf smiled. "Good. You like to read?"

"Well, duh. Why else would I work in a bookstore?" I hesitated, then decided to jump in with both feet. "I've read all the books you bought today," I said. "I like mysteries, particularly ones with gay or lesbian characters. I like to see myself and the people I know represented in the books I read."

"I do, too," he said. "Like mysteries. There is something very satisfying about seeing a detective risk everything to make the world right."

I noticed he skimmed right over the gay comment, and I wished I had my laptop there so I could Google him before the conversation went much farther. If you put "prince," "Eisengraf," and "gay" together, would you get any results?

Wolf lifted his glass. "To books. And conversation about them."

I clinked my glass against his. He was setting the parameters of the evening. Since he was paying for dinner, that was his right.

We compared notes on books we'd read. He had studied with private tutors as a child, reading many of the great classics and discussing them. "My sister is a year older than I am," he said. "So we studied together."

"And college?"

"Oxford." That explained the overlay of a British accent. "My mother died when I was six, and my father, he was busy running the country. He was something of a snob, you know, and we did not associate with ordinary children. It was lonely there in the castle, with only my sister as my friend."

The waiter brought our soup, and we dug in. "And you?" he asked. "What did you read as a child, besides Welsh folktales?"

"Whatever I could get my hands on," I said. "My mom worked long hours, and I'd go to the library after school and wait for her to pick me up. The librarian turned me on to the classic British mysteries—Christie, Allingham, Sayers. After that, I just ranged through the shelves and picked out anything that interested me."

The soup was delicious, and it was comfortable talking to Wolf. "What brings you to Florida?" I asked. "Vacation?"

"A bit," he said. "I am speaking to a group tomorrow evening in Coral Gables. Perspectives on governance in the New Europe. Not very interesting, I am afraid. But we have a legislature, and a prime minister in Eisengraf, so my office is largely ceremonial."

"You said your sister was older," I said. "Why isn't she the princess regent?"

"There is no such office," he said. "The treaty with Kaiser Wilhelm is very specific. A male heir is required. If neither my sister nor I provide one, Eisengraf ceases to exist as an independent principality, and all control cedes to Germany."

"Does your sister have any sons?"

"She only married a year ago," Wolf said. "So far she has not become pregnant. But if she has a son, that will remove the pressure on me. If she does not, then it will be up to me to provide an heir to the throne."

As I considered what that meant, Wolf steered the conversation back to books. The waiter arrived with the lobsters and the side dishes, and we dug in. The food was delicious, the beer excellent. I tried to shut off the analytical part of my brain and just enjoy dinner with this handsome, charming man who loved books as much as I did.

I kept trying to read signs in his speech and posture. He had to be gay. I'd been out of the dating pool for a while, but I wasn't dense. But was he flirting with me? Every now and then our eyes would meet, and he would smile, and I'd feel a tingle run through my groin. But at the same time, he was so formal, so restrained.

We ordered coffee and dessert. Wolf seemed reluctant to let the evening end, and I was happy to stay with him. He intrigued me. And he made me feel things in parts of my body I thought had been put out of commission permanently.

By the time he asked for the check, I knew I would have to be the one to make a move. But how?

"I imagine that discretion must be very important to you," I said, after he'd handed the waiter his black American Express card. "I know a lot of guys who would kiss and tell—but that's not me. I know how to keep a secret."

He quirked his eyebrows up but didn't say anything. I plowed on. I was either about to embarrass myself or get Wolf into bed. But I couldn't stop. "I live just a few blocks from the bookstore." I lowered my voice and leaned toward him. "It's not much, but it's very private. If you wanted to take a walk up there with me, no one would have to know."

Wolf's body was as taut as a plucked violin string. I worried that I'd gone too far, that I'd get an icy no thank you. But then his shoulders eased, and he said, "I don't get the chance to see much ordinary life," he said. "I would like that. To come to your apartment. Very much."

I smiled at him, and got a smile in return. Not the saturnine grin I had seen before, but something shyer. Sweeter. Oh, my, I thought.

We didn't talk as we walked down Lincoln Road, or even as we turned down the side street that led to my apartment. When we were a block away, Wolf said, "I don't want to mislead you."

I stopped and turned to him. "In what way?"

He looked at a loss for words.

"I have limited expectations," I said. "I would like to kiss you, once we're behind closed doors. Is that something you would like, too?"

He shifted uncomfortably, but looked at me. "Yes."

"Then you're not misleading me at all."

My apartment is a mother-in-law unit attached to an art deco house. I have my own entrance behind the garage. It's not much of a place—a sitting room with a galley kitchen, and a bedroom and bathroom. I flipped the light switch, ushered Wolf inside, and then followed him in.

"Very charming," he said.

"Not exactly a castle."

"A castle can be a very cold place," he said. "Not much of a home."

I dropped my keys on the table next to the door and took

Wolf's hand in mine. His was cold and damp, despite the heat of the evening. We were almost the same height, so when I turned my face to him our lips met without difficulty. At first he did not respond, but then he put his arm around my back and leaned toward me. His lips were cool and dry, but his dark eyes blazed as I looked right into them.

His kiss was delicate, just the lightest pressure on my lips. But when I pushed my body against his, I felt his hardness through his elegantly tailored pants. I brushed my hand against it as I pulled back. "I've been a bad host," I said. "I haven't even offered you anything."

"You have offered," he said, smiling. "I would like very much to accept."

"I like the way you think."

I began to unbutton his starched white shirt. His body tensed again, and I said, "Don't worry, I'll be sure not to wrinkle it."

He laughed, and his posture relaxed a little. "That is not ..."

"You're not a virgin, are you?" I asked, pulling his shirttails out of his pants and letting his shirt hang loosely. "Not as handsome as you are."

"No. Not a virgin. But this is not...it is not something I do lightly."

"That's sweet." I slipped the shirt off, folded it, and laid it on top of my sofa. When I turned back to him he had crossed his arms in front of his chest. "If it makes you feel any better, you're the first man I've been with in over a year."

"So long?" He reached out and put his hand around my head, and pulled us together. "Sadly, it has been more than that for me."

We kissed again, and this time Wolf put more feeling into it. His lips pressed against mine, his eyes closed, and his body relaxed another few degrees. I pulled back, slipped my T-shirt

off over my head, then unbuttoned my shorts and let them drop
to the floor. I kicked off my deck shoes and stood there wearing
only a pair of boxer shorts patterned with sea horses.

I pulled Wolf close to me and nuzzled the hollow of his neck.
His body sagged and I lowered my head to his right nipple,
which I kissed and licked. He made a small whimpering sound,
which I took to mean that he liked what I was doing.

I kept on doing it, first to his right nipple, then to his left.
Then he pulled back from me, smiling. "You make me feel over-
dressed." He unbuckled his belt—a Louis Vuitton, I noticed—
and then kicked off his dress shoes. He stepped out of his slacks,
folded them, and laid them over the sofa next to his shirt.

As he turned I gaped at his body. He was easily the handsomest man I'd ever had in front of me who wasn't on a computer
screen or on the pages of a magazine. His broad chest tapered
to a narrow waist, and his slim legs were strong and muscular.
His white briefs hugged his body, outlining a stiff dick with a
circumcised mushroom head.

He bent over to pull off his black socks. When he stood
again, he said, "There. Now I feel we are more equal."

I just stood there with my mouth hanging open.

"Is there something wrong?"

I shook my head. "You're so handsome. I can't believe you're
real."

He stepped in close to me, and I inhaled the lemon of his
aftershave. "I am real. Let me show you."

This time, he kissed me like he meant it. Our bodies melded
together, the narrow trail of dark hair that ran down his chest
soft and silky against my skin. I put my hands on his ass and
held him close.

His briefs were a fine cotton, molded to his butt cheeks, but
I snaked my hands under the waistband and cupped his butt,

pressing my stiff dick against his. Then I leaned back a little. "I have a bed. Let me show it to you."

I took his hand and led him into the bedroom, where I shucked my boxers and got down on my knees. I pulled down the waistband of his briefs and his dick popped out. He groaned as I took him in my mouth.

After a minute or two, he sat down on the edge of the bed, and I rested my hands on the mattress as I sucked him. He began to pant and shiver and pulled my head off his dick. He scooted back on the bed and motioned for me to join him.

We kissed and cuddled, then he slid down to take my dick in his mouth. He'd done that a few times, I could tell. I loved the way his tongue slid up and down the length of my dick, the gentle suction he applied when he sucked me. I pulled back, just for a minute, so that I could scoot around, and we were dick to mouth and mouth to dick.

It didn't take long for us both to come to the brink of orgasm that way. He pulled off me first, circling my dick with his hand as he jerked me, and I did the same to him. I came first, shuddering, feeling the power of my lust flowing through my whole body, and he followed soon after.

I clambered out of bed, went into the bathroom, and returned a moment later with a damp towel, which I used to clean us both up. Then I dropped the towel on the bedside table and got back into bed next to Wolf.

He'd shucked his briefs while I was in the bathroom, and we lay there next to each other, naked, not talking. Our heads rested on the pillows, facing each other, and he smiled. I smiled back, then lifted myself up on one elbow. "You are so handsome."

"You are the sun," he said. "So blond, so happy and bright. It is you who are the most handsome, my friend."

I was a cute kid. Adorable, if you want the truth. I look at pictures of that little blond boy and see that. I went through an awkward phase as a teenager, putting on some weight, affecting a wispy mustache that I imagined made me look older.

When I got to college, I jumped out of the closet, and I found the best place to pick up guys was the locker room at the gym. So I took up swimming, and as my body slimmed my number of conquests grew. By the time I graduated I had that proverbial swimmer's build—but also a reputation as a slut.

Wolf sat up. "I should go. I have to make an early start tomorrow."

"I thought your speech was in the evening?"

"I am being interviewed on the radio," he said. "Eight-fifteen, I think. And then breakfast with a very wealthy Eisengraf couple who live in Coral Gables. Lunch with a man who owns a bank, and then an interview in the afternoon with the Miami *Herald*."

"Busy day." I reached out to run a finger gently down his chest. "Will you have any free time before you have to leave?"

He shook his head, and it felt like my heart had fallen to the pit of my stomach. "I have already pledged all my free time," he said. "To a very charming man I met in a bookstore."

I slapped my hand lightly on his chest. "You're a big tease, is what you are."

He laughed. "Tomorrow, I must attend this dreary dinner and play the royal prince. But I can already feel a headache coming on as it draws to a close, perhaps eight o'clock. Is it possible you would be free after that?"

"It's possible," I said.

"You understand, I must be discreet," he said. "The American tabloids, they are vicious. I see the scandals they build out of the most innocent behavior."

"Your behavior tonight has hardly been innocent."

He plowed on. "I would invite you to this dinner, if I could. It would lighten my heart to see you there. And I would invite you to come to my hotel, to stay with me, and make love there...."

"But you can't. I understand. Can you find your way back here tomorrow night, after your dinner is over?"

He smiled. "I can do that."

I offered to walk him back to his car, parked in a lot near the bookstore, but he said he could find his way. He dressed carefully, checking his reflection in the bedroom mirror to make sure he didn't look like he'd just rolled out of bed.

We kissed once more before he left. "Let me give you my phone number," I said. "In case you get delayed, or something comes up. I have a class at ten tomorrow morning, but I'll be at the bookstore from twelve to five."

He slid the piece of paper into his wallet. Leather. Hermès, I thought. I closed the door firmly behind him. The next morning I woke a little after sunrise and walked over to the beach. I swam in the ocean as I did most days, out and back in, then parallel to the shore and back. I stopped at the bank to deposit my paycheck and heard Wolf's voice being interviewed on the local radio station.

He was about halfway through his interview, talking about politics and the EEC. Eisengraf was a member of the European Union, had accepted the euro as its currency, and opened its borders to member nations.

I hung around the bank until the interview was over. I wasted a few minutes on my walk home thinking of Wolf, wondering if he would think of me at all. But then I had to shower and dress and get ready for my class.

The day passed quickly between teaching and working at the bookstore. I didn't want to think too much about Wolf, because I was worried that he might not show up again, especially if I wanted him to. He had told me he was busy, and I could easily imagine him calling to say he was unable to get out of his dinner, that he was leaving the next day for Eisengraf, that it had been wonderful to meet me.

I made my own dinner, rice and veggies, a cheap meal that was nothing at all like my wonderful meal with Wolf the night before. I willed myself not to look at the clock and wonder if Wolf would show up or not.

At nine, my phone rang. "I am so sorry, Rhys," Wolf said. "As I feared, I was unable to escape my dinner obligation so easily. But there is good news."

"Really? What's that?"

"I have agreed to chair a commission investigating a common currency for Latin America, similar to the euro."

I wanted to say, and that matters to me because... But I was being polite. "Congratulations."

"This commission will do its work here in Miami," Wolf said. "So I will be staying here for some time."

My heart jumped. "That is good news."

"We must celebrate. I am leaving Coral Gables now, but it will take me some time to reach you. I wanted to make sure it was acceptable to arrive so late."

I laughed. "It would be more than acceptable," I said.

We hung up and I began pacing around the apartment. What did this mean? Would Wolf and I begin dating? What about Eisengraf? Didn't he have responsibilities back there?

I was still pacing when I heard the knock on my front door. I opened it to find Wolf holding a bottle of champagne and two long-stemmed glasses. "Wow! When you said celebrate you really meant it."

He grinned broadly as he stepped inside. "There is more

good news," he said. "I spoke with my sister earlier today."

I led him to the kitchen, where he expertly uncorked the bottle of champagne, pouring it into the two glasses.

"To my sister," he said, lifting his glass. "Princess Hannah-Sophie. And to the boy child she carries in her womb."

"Congratulations," I said, tipping my glass against his. "So that means…"

"That means that I may live openly as I wish," Wolf said. "Of course, I must be discreet. I do not plan to ride a float in the Gay Pride Parade in Berlin. But I can take an apartment here in Miami and invite any man I wish to visit me there."

He looked deep into my eyes, and I felt a shiver go up my spine. "Or to live there with me, if a relationship should grow in that way."

I put aside my glass and leaned toward Wolf, and his lips met mine in a kiss that was part passion, part need, and part joy. I wanted to open up my computer, head to Facebook, and post a comment on Elaina's page, telling her that I'd been right all along. But that would have to wait; I had my handsome prince in my arms and it was going to be a long time before I let him go.

CHAUFFEUR PRINCE

Bonnie Dee

G ary pulled the cab to the curb, muscling in between a BMW and an Audi. His fare stood awaiting him on the sidewalk. At least he assumed the tall man with blond-streaked dark-brown hair was the one who'd called for a ride. Gary leaned across the seat. "Albertson?"

The man bent and peered in at him through the open window, the pungent smell of alcohol wafting from him in an invisible cloud. "In the flesh."

The drawled tone of privilege grated against Gary's ears like fingernails on a chalkboard. A piss-drunk, Harvard-educated waste of space. He knew the type too well. Too much money and not a clue about living a real life.

As the fare tumbled into the back seat and slammed the door, Gary stole a glimpse at him in the rearview. Even drunk, the man looked like a fucking GQ model. His hair was beautifully tousled, his tie askew, and his black suit rumpled but exquisitely tailored.

Albertson met his gaze in the mirror. Their eyes locked as they weighed each other for a prolonged moment, sending *that* message—attraction. Gary had spent a lifetime making silent connections like this. But this guy was not a pickup. He was a job. That was all. Turning his eyes to the street, Gary pulled away from the curb and into late-night traffic.

"Where to?" he asked.

"Home, James." An annoying bark of laughter came from the back seat. "I don't care. Just drive for a while."

Fine, he'd circle the block a few times, rack up some mileage while this guy made up his mind. For a few minutes there was blissful silence as he turned at the next corner and the next. He'd happily drive all night while Sleeping Beauty snored in the back seat.

A low groan from his passenger snapped his attention back to the rearview.

"Hey, man, don't puke in the cab."

"Not puking." Albertson grunted, pushing himself upright. His head and shoulders bobbed into view as he leaned against the front seat. It was an old-fashioned cab with no safety glass separating driver from passenger.

Gary glanced at Albertson's profile, chiseled features, high-bridged nose, sculpted cheekbones, full lips. It wasn't right that a man should have wealth, power, privilege, and beauty too.

"So, Gary Rowe," Albertson read his name off the ID badge on the dash, "what's your story? How'd you land a job like this? You must meet a lot of shitheels in your line of work."

"When I'm on the night shift," Gary said dryly. "All the drunks are out in full force."

"You don't drink?" Albertson leaned a little closer. A whiff of woodsy cologne mingled with the alcohol vapors. The man smelled good and despite himself, Gary felt his cock twitch.

"Sure. I throw back a few. But I know my limit."

"You'd never puke in a cab."

"That's right."

Gary reached another corner and signaled another right turn, but his passenger rested a hand on his shoulder and pointed. "That way. Go toward the river."

Flicking off the signal, he merged out of the turn lane.

Albertson sat back and rummaged in his jacket pocket for something. Gary watched in the mirror as the man pulled out a baggie and papers and started to roll. He kept his mouth shut. He could air out the cab before he took on another passenger or returned it to the garage.

"How long you been driving?" Albertson asked. "Do you like it?"

"Hours are flexible. Pays the bills. It's all right." Gary watched the deft way those long fingers rolled the joint and brought it to his mouth, the way Albertson's lips pursed around it and his hands cupped the lighter. Each simple movement plucked at Gary's libido and made him hotter. He dragged his attention back to the road.

"Maybe that's what I need, to find a simple job that pays the bills." Albertson sucked a deep lungful of smoke and held it.

Gary didn't answer. He doubted Albertson needed to work at all. Now that he'd had time to think about it, he recognized the famous last name and the face he'd seen on tabloid covers in the checkout line. This was Hale Albertson, black sheep of *the* Albertson family, living off the family teat and celebrating life in high style as only a spoiled rich boy could.

Albertson reached across the seat and offered him the joint. Gary shook his head.

"You don't smoke either?"

"Not while I'm driving."

"Then pull over. There's a place you can park near the river, a great view and nobody bothers you."

Gary knew the spot, and what went on there. He'd indulged in a few chance meetings there himself, back when he'd been younger, wilder, and interested in nothing more than sex, sex, and more sex. Not that he was old now, but at almost thirty he simply wasn't looking for brainless satisfaction any longer.

Apparently Albertson was, and he'd decided Gary might provide it tonight.

Gary drew a deep breath and inhaled the sharp burn of pot. He should shut this party down right now. Drop Albertson off somewhere before they both got busted and he lost his job.

He should. But he found himself turning onto a side street and then another, pulling into a parking lot sheltered by some straggly trees and an abandoned building. Not the safest part of town. The cab's headlights flashed across the rippling river, illuminating the water and making it pretty rather than polluted, if you ignored the garbage along the edge.

Gary cut the lights but left the engine purring—and the meter running.

Another car was parked at the far side of the lot, lights off, no movement inside. The place was deserted tonight. Likely everyone who was looking for a quick fuck was someplace sensible like a club.

"Here." Albertson offered him the weed again.

This time Gary took it and inhaled before passing it back.

"What do you want?" he asked and realized he sounded like a $20 whore. That wasn't what he'd meant.

"A man of business. Right to the point. I like that."

"No. I'm not here to fuck around. I meant, what is it you're looking for?"

Albertson raised his brows as he coughed out a cloud of smoke. "I'd think that would be fairly obvious."

"If you want some action, I can drop you off at Chez Salome

or any place on Carbon Street." Gary's voice sounded huskier than normal, his throat seared by the smoke. He hadn't indulged in a long time.

"I'm not dressed for clubbing. Besides I can't stand the noise and running into the same boys every week. Shit. Maybe it's time for a European trip. Try something different."

Gary couldn't suppress a derisive snort. Must be nice to change things up and fly off to a foreign country when you got bored with life.

"You think I'm a real dick, don't you?" Albertson laughed. "You'd be right." He took another drag before offering the joint to Gary again. "Go ahead. Lay it out for me. Tell me how shallow and self-centered I am."

Ooh, that was too tempting. The strong weed was already clouding his judgment. Gary didn't bite down on his tongue this time. Screw the tip.

"Did you ever think maybe the 'something new' you're searching for can't be found outside of yourself? Maybe you're what needs to change."

"Deep. But not a singular opinion. I've heard something like it before from my therapist." How was it possible for someone to sound amused and bitter at the same time?

Gary shrugged. "My two cents, but what do I know? Now, where can I take you?"

"I'll pay you a thousand bucks not to ask me that again. Come on." Albertson opened the car door and was out of the vehicle before Gary knew what was happening.

"Shit!" For a split second he considered driving off and leaving the guy. Cut his losses and carry on with his evening. But he climbed out of the car and stood leaning on the open door, watching the other man shamble toward the water's edge. "Hey. What are you doing?"

Albertson looked over his shoulder, his face pale in the moonlight, his eyes glittering. "Not drowning myself. Don't worry."

He picked something up and chucked it at the water. It landed with a splash.

"Shit," Gary said again. He couldn't turn the engine off. There'd be time lost on his meter. But he didn't want to leave the cab running while he chased after Albertson.

He left the door ajar and walked toward the river and his wayward passenger. "Why don't you come back to the car?"

"Why don't you come wade in the water?" Albertson was taking off his shoes.

"Don't do that. It's filthy and you could cut your foot." Gary hurried over and seized the man's arm before he shied the shoe into the water. "For God's sake, get a grip."

Gary took the shoe and tossed it on the ground, then grabbed Albertson's arms and pulled him back from the water's edge. "You're crazy."

"No. Just bored."

"And stupid." He pulled Albertson up against him, wrapping his arms around him. The man's back was against his chest. Every solid inch of him pressed hard against Gary, and Gary's solid inches rubbed against his ass.

"What's your problem anyway? Daddy didn't give you enough attention so you act out?" he snarled, trying to cover for his undeniable arousal.

"Something like that." Albertson didn't even sound annoyed at the assessment. It was as if he knew he was a walking cliché and had given up caring.

Suddenly Gary felt bad for judging this man's life without knowing a thing about it. Hadn't he suffered enough of that judgment focused in his direction?

"Look, you'll feel better in the morning. Why don't we get

in the car now? I'll take you to a diner and buy you a cup of coffee."

The other man sagged against him and let out a sigh. Gary supported his weight, slinging one of Albertson's arms around his neck and guiding him back to the cab. He leaned him against it and hurried back to get the abandoned shoe.

When he returned, Albertson was sitting on the trunk of the cab, leaning against the rear window, staring up at the sky. "Have you ever been in the desert? The stars are amazing there. You can see every single one."

"My family used to go camping in the mountains. Same thing. I haven't been out of the city in years." Gary flashed back to a time when he hadn't had to worry about money or bills or responsibilities.

He stood in front of Albertson and took hold of his ankle. He slipped the expensive leather shoe on the other man's foot and began to tie it, then glanced up and met Hale Albertson's eyes watching him. Suddenly the act of lacing the shoe seemed much more intimate.

Gary's breath caught and his pulse sped up.

"Sit with me," Albertson said.

"Aw, Jesus," Gary muttered, but climbed onto the trunk. He leaned back against the cool windshield, shoulder to shoulder with his passenger, and looked up at the sky. Only a few feeble stars pierced the smog and shone against the yellow glow from the city lights. The engine and headlights of the car at the far end of the lot suddenly came on. A few seconds later the vehicle drove away, leaving them alone in the secluded spot.

"What do you do? I mean, other than drive a taxi?" Albertson asked.

"I'm taking college courses."

"And what'll you be when you're finished, Gary? It is Gary,

right?" He stuck out a hand. "I'm Hale."

Gary shook his hand, the warmth of skin against skin reminding him of other body parts that could rub together. "Yeah, I know."

Hale withdrew his hand slowly before lacing it with the other across his flat stomach. "My infamy precedes me."

"The party prince, heir to the Albertson fortune? I've heard your reputation, but I don't know who you are."

"I'm everything they say and worse. But I want to know about you, Gary Rowe. What are your hopes and aspirations?"

Gary hesitated. His wasn't an exciting career choice but it was important to him and he didn't really want to hear some rich dude sneer at it. "I'm almost finished earning my teaching degree."

"You want to teach?" Hale turned his head to look at him. "That's admirable given the hell schools are these days."

"Early elementary. Not high school. I like little kids." The statement hung in dead space sounding perverted. "They're honest. No hidden agendas."

"I get that," Hale agreed. "Although I don't know if I personally could stand a classroom full of screaming five-year-olds."

"No worse than dealing with drunks at three in the morning."

Albertson laughed, a real, full-bodied laugh rather than the sardonic chuckles Gary had heard from him so far.

"Absofuckinglutely. Although I have to tell you, I'm not all that drunk." Hale snaked a hand out and rested it on Gary's thigh. "Not too drunk to get busy."

Gary stared at the hand, well manicured, heavy and warm on his leg, and considered removing it—or moving it onto the bulge in his jeans. Instead, he ignored it and changed the subject. "What about you? What are your future plans?"

"If I knew, I wouldn't be here at three in the morning coming on to some taxi driver who's clearly not interested."

Oh, I'm interested all right, Gary wanted to protest.

"I have a couple of half-finished degrees," Hale continued, "but I suppose I'll end up working for my father's corporation some day. Can't put him off forever."

"Nothing wrong with that." Gary nodded. He'd worked with his father for a while before he'd sold the store, but the old man had driven him crazy. "If that's what you really want. But when you close your eyes and think about what makes you happiest, what do you see?"

Hale closed his eyes, long lashes resting against his cheeks. Gary wanted to reach out and touch them with the tip of his finger. He studied the man's profile, the handsome elegance so different from his own squared-off, blunt features. Gary had often thought he could easily blend in if he were transported back in time to the Polish countryside of his peasant forbears. Strong genes on both sides gave him an Old Country look.

Hale's eyes remained closed for so long, Gary thought he might've fallen asleep.

"What would you wish for if you could have anything?" he prodded.

"Are you my fairy godmother?" the man murmured sleepily.

"Say I am, just for tonight. What would make you happy?"

"A blow job." One eyelid slowly rose and Hale smirked at him.

Gary stared back, not accepting the blithe response. "A blow job makes every man happy. Now give me a real answer."

Hale nodded an acknowledgment of his asshattedness and paused to consider before replying. "I like to sail. I'm happy when I'm out on my boat. But that's recreation, not something to devote your life to."

"Not if you run a charter business. You could make it a career," Gary pointed out.

"You're chock full of good advice, aren't you?"

"All part of the service," Gary said. "Remember it when you give me my tip."

Hale laughed again, the warm chuckle not the mirthless bray, and Gary smiled back at him. There they sat, two strangers on the trunk of a car, connecting over a few shared confidences and a little teasing.

"What else?" Gary asked. "Deep in your heart, what do you think would bring you joy?"

Hale frowned. "I don't know. Sometimes I don't know if real joy is possible. There's always that sense of something missing, a desire for"—he cast around, searching for the words—"for something more."

Gary nodded. "Something more." *Or maybe someone.*

Their gazes locked as they had earlier in the rearview mirror, a deep piercing catch, like a hook sliding into a fish's mouth and digging in hard.

Hale leaned toward him. Gary inclined his head, half-closing his eyes as the other man's face filled his vision. And then a warm mouth covered his, a tongue pressed between his lips, and Hale slipped a hand around the back of his neck, pulling him even closer.

The kiss tasted sour and herbal, liquor and pot combined with Hale's own flavor. His insistent tongue plunged into Gary's mouth, demanding and searching. Gary gripped Hale's jacket, then pushed it off his shoulder and slid a palm over the smooth cotton of his shirt, feeling the muscles beneath.

His cock strained against his jeans and pressed against Hale's leg as Gary sprawled half on top of him. He rocked his hips but it gave him no relief. He needed flesh against flesh, a hand gripping his cock. Mindless lust took over, giving the lie to his earlier belief that he didn't like or need casual encounters any longer. He thought he'd grown beyond them, but here he was lolling on the back of a car, dry humping a stranger.

Hale groaned and slid a hand up Gary's back beneath his T-shirt, singeing every bit of skin it touched. Gary whimpered in response, a soft sound that was embarrassing in its neediness. He dragged his mouth away from Hale's and gasped for air.

Smoky dark eyes gazed into his from inches away and Hale snaked a hand down in between them to unfasten Gary's fly. He reached inside and freed Gary's cock, wrapping a hot palm around the shaft and pulling with sharp tugs that made Gary gasp.

Gary straddled the other man, planting a knee on either side of him, risking the metal plate buckling beneath their combined weight. He groped the front of Hale's black trousers, touching the ridge beneath and sliding his hand up. He unbuckled Hale's belt and opened his fly to reveal a pair of gray briefs. The bulge was even more pronounced. Gary tugged down the waistband, freeing his thick erection.

Although the parking lot was shadowy, there was enough light for him to see the length and girth of the other man's cock as he encircled it in his fist. It felt smooth and hard and hot as he slid his hand up and down the shaft. They faced each other, hands gripping each other's dicks, stroking and offering mutual pleasure.

Friction heated his palm as he moved his hand fast up and down Hale's cock. Hard to keep up the rhythm when his own pleasure was growing and he was losing focus. Gary groaned as Hale massaged his cock in steady strokes, matching his speed and the strength of his pulling.

Gary's knuckles grazed against the ginger tangle of Hale's

hair and the warmth of his belly with every downstroke. Gary wished he could see more than a tantalizing glimpse of the man's taut abdomen. He'd like to have him spread out naked beneath him. He'd like to take his time and suck him off and then bury his cock in what was doubtless a toned, tight ass.

Hale's hips bucked as he pushed himself into Gary's fist. His eyes were nearly closed and his lips parted, his head tilted back so the dim light illuminated the pleasure on his face. "Oh yeah," he muttered. "Yeah."

Gary gazed down at him. *Beautiful. You're beautiful. And maybe not as much of an asshole as I thought at first. Just a lost and rootless soul searching for a friend.*

And then conscious thought left him as primal desire unfurled deep in his groin, lashing out like vines, binding his balls tight and shooting up through his penis. Hale's hand gripping his shaft conjured the elemental force, bringing it to the surface and sending Gary soaring to climax.

He let out a guttural grunt as cum spilled from him, shooting over Hale's hand and spattering his shirt. Gary's eyes closed and ecstasy rolled through him, but he remembered to keep pumping. He could hear from Hale's panting breaths and increased moans that he was close, too.

"Oh God, yesss," Hale hissed and Gary opened his eyes to watch him cum.

The other man's face was contorted with pleasure. Gary felt the throbbing of the cock in his fist as Hale released in steady spurts. The only sounds were their jagged breathing, the continual hum of traffic and the steady rush of the river flowing by.

When Gary was certain the last wave of orgasm had passed through Hale, he released his cock. It thumped softly against the other man's belly.

Hale let go of him, and Gary wiped up as best he could with

the tail of his T-shirt, then tucked himself away. The aftermath of these brief encounters was always a letdown. Toys back in the box, and the boys hurried off to play other games. Gary remembered why he'd stopped doing stuff like this.

He climbed off the back of the car and held out a hand to help Hale down.

The cab was still purring, exhaust fumes spurting out the tailpipe, the meter running, and the two men stood facing each other in an empty parking lot.

"Is that what you wanted?" Gary asked.

"What else is there? We could go back to my apartment if you'd like, take it a little farther, a little deeper." Hale grinned, making the double entendre obvious.

Gary could picture a penthouse apartment, likely the entire top floor of one of Albertson Senior's buildings. Views of the city from every window. Furnishings so expensive that a mere end table would probably cost about month's worth of his wages. A state-of-the-art kitchen. A massive bed two guys could use for a playground, probably with a closet full of toys and props. He could picture Hale living in such a place, a big-boy bachelor pad, full of creature comforts but lacking in a deeper kind of comfort.

If he accepted the offer, they'd have more sex and it would be good. Then they'd say good-bye in the morning and the ball would be over. Gary knew instinctively that wasn't what Hale needed.

It wasn't what *he* needed.

He looked at his watch. "I'm not off the clock for another couple of hours."

"Take the cab back. Tell 'em you're sick. I'll pay for your time."

Gary stared at him. The guy didn't even seem to realize he'd basically asked him to whore himself.

"I've got a better idea. We'll pick up some coffee and share it while I drive you around the city. We'll talk. And when my shift's over, after I turn in the car, we'll go out for breakfast."

"A date?" Hale raised a quizzical eyebrow.

"Yeah. A date."

"No fucking?"

"Not this time," Gary said firmly. "We'll get to know each other first and see how it goes. I'm willing to hold out for the 'something more.'"

Hale smiled. "That sounds good."

Gary opened the car door and held it while his fare climbed inside. He closed the door behind Hale and climbed into the driver's seat.

Then he whisked the prince away in his carriage toward a happily ever after.

THE PRINCE
OF TIRES

Heidi Champa

S tacy and Rob sure knew how to throw a party. Well, at least they always supplied enough free booze. God bless them for moving into a new house. Not that we needed an excuse to get together and drink, but as we've gotten older and hit thirty, it seemed classier to have a reason to get shit-faced. I had a policy that whatever I spent on a gift for a party, I tried to drink the equivalent amount in booze. That way, everyone was happy.

I knew there was no way I could drive home; we were too far out in the country to get a cab. But I couldn't stay over, because I had to be up too early the next morning. I was struck with a brilliant idea—at least it seemed brilliant to my wine-soaked brain. Using the fancy roadside assistance button in my car, I summoned a tow truck to Stacy and Rob's driveway. The tinny, female voice told me to sit tight and help would arrive soon.

Everyone else had left the party and Stacy and Rob had gone to bed. I sat on the stone wall that lined the driveway, staring up at the sky when I heard the rumbling engine coming down the

road. I looked up and was nearly blinded by the orange lights
flashing on top of the white truck. It lit up the whole driveway,
making it look like daytime. The strobe effect of the lights was
making my head hurt, but I didn't want to let the driver know I
was drunk, so I tried to pull it together before he saw me.

The driver jumped out from the cab, and I got up and walked
toward him, trying my damnedest not to stagger. He shook his
head when he saw me coming, his face showing his agitation.
Despite his scowl, I could tell right away how attractive he was.

"What seems to be the trouble with the car?"

"Oh, I'm not sure. It wouldn't start. I think it's the battery or
maybe the transmission."

"Right. Does it start at all?"

"Sometimes, but not all the time. I didn't think I should risk
it. You can help me, right?"

I stopped talking just in time for a loud hiccup to leave my
mouth. It was followed by a burp, and the noise made me giggle.
I wasn't doing a very good job of hiding my condition. He shook
his head again, and I thought I saw a smirk cross his lips. I was
still buzzed, but not nearly as drunk as I had been earlier in the
night. His voice was deep, and had an authority to it that made
me jump, and made my cock harden a bit.

"Well, no problem. I can tow it to your garage for you and
they can figure it out."

"It's not going to a garage, it's going to my house. I'll deal
with it on my own. If that's okay?"

He didn't ask me any more questions, just turned to do his
work. I looked closer at him, watching him trussing up my
car and mutter to himself. His rust-colored hair was short but
messy, falling over his forehead as he strapped my wheels to the
moving flatbed. His green buttoned-down shirt had the sleeves
rolled up, and his freckled forearms flexed as he worked the

controls, sliding my car up onto its new high perch.

He was cute, in a blue-collar kind of way. He wasn't the typical tow truck driver, or my usual type, but my body was reacting strongly, overruling my logical brain. I felt my cock stir again as I watched him, his jeans sinking low on his hips as he stretched and bent to secure my car. When he stood up and licked his lips absentmindedly, I lost my breath for a second. It was weird. I hadn't felt an instant zing from anyone in a long time. Leave it to me to find it in a tow truck driver in the middle of the night.

Once the truck stopped moving, the quiet returned, the profound silence broken by his footsteps crunching on the gravel driveway. He stopped about a foot away from me and tried to meet my eyes, but I couldn't focus. I heard him loudly sniffing, and then he laughed.

"There's nothing wrong with your car, is there buddy? You're drunk."

"No I'm not. Well, maybe a little bit. My name is Scott, by the way."

"I should report you, you know. Tow trucks are for people who are stranded, not party boys who are too stupid to crash on a friend's couch. It's not like I don't have better things to do with my night."

"I'm not stupid, I'm actually very clever. I'm a lawyer, and technically what I'm doing isn't against the law, you know. So, how about that ride? I'm very nice, once you get to know me."

"You're very something, that's for sure."

"And, you're very cute."

He didn't say anything, just smiled a bit and rubbed his hand against his chin. I felt the awkwardness growing in the silence between us, so I decided to keep talking to try and make it go away.

"Sorry I ruined your evening. Maybe I can pay you back someday. You know, for rescuing me."

I couldn't believe I had said it, and I felt the flush creeping up my cheeks. My words had the opposite effect on the awkwardness, and I felt even lamer than I did after calling him cute. The name on his shirt said Beau, but I decided it didn't suit him. His eyes were framed by thick lashes and the freckles that were on his arms also covered his face. It may have been the alcohol in my blood, but I could have sworn I saw his eyes roaming over me, just for a few seconds. His voice wobbled a bit from trying to hide his laughter, but his words made me melt just a bit.

"I don't think a clever boy like you needs to be rescued. But, I'm sure I can think of a way for you to make it up to me."

My throat seized up for a minute, but I ignored it and kept talking.

"I know this wasn't the smartest plan, but give me credit for trying."

"You really can talk your way out of anything, can't you Scott?"

"It's what I do. But, most of the time, I just convince people to do something they already wanted to do. They just don't know it yet."

He smiled and I stumbled forward, his hands grasping my shoulders to keep me up. I waited for him to push me away, but he didn't. Our faces were close together, and I did something even stupider than a drunk dialing a tow truck. I kissed him.

He didn't stop me. In fact, after a few seconds, he put a hand around my neck, pushing his tongue deeper into my mouth. He wasn't new to kissing men, too confident to just be a curious guy taking advantage of my drunken state. My brain ran through a thousand different thoughts but couldn't fix on any of them. He pulled back, a strong hand still on my shoulder. A bit of panic hit me, and I started trying to explain.

"Shit. I'm sorry. I don't know why I did that."

"Yes, you do. Unless you're drunker than I thought, you're flirting with me pretty hard. You even called me cute. You are too, by the way, in case you were wondering."

I was blushing more than I had since high school, feeling like a teenager again. I tried to cover, but it failed completely.

"I just didn't want you to call the cops."

"Right. Whatever you say. Let's go, Romeo."

He walked me slowly toward the truck and helped me into the passenger's side. His hand ran over my back as I climbed inside, sending a shiver down my spine. I waited patiently as he walked around the truck, and we rode in silence back to my house, his hand resting on my knee the whole way. I tried not to fall as I exited the cab, the height providing more of a challenge than I thought. He lowered my car into the driveway, and I fumbled with my keys, trying to find the right one. I could hear the laughter in his voice, his face hidden by the shadows.

"Having a little trouble there? Let me help you."

It was dark, and despite my rapidly clearing head, every task seemed to be more difficult than usual. My boy Beau followed me to the front door, grabbing the keys from my clumsy hands. I was about to protest when his lips were back on mine, pushing me gently until my back hit the door. His knee slipped between my thighs, and I rocked my hips forward into his.

Things heated up, hands roaming under clothes, so Beau broke our kiss and tried a few keys before letting us inside. He was patient as I walked us slowly to the bedroom, stopping every few feet to get another luscious taste of his mouth. Our clothes started to fall, leaving a trail down the long hall of my second floor. I felt the need to explain, a tiny pang of guilt getting through my fading alcohol cloud.

"Beau, I don't usually do this kind of thing."

"Me neither, Scott. But, sometimes things happen for a reason. You don't have to question it."

"Can't help it, that's what I do."

I stood at the foot of my bed and let him pull my pants down. He took his time removing my shoes and socks, kissing randomly on my legs, stroking my kneecaps with his tongue. It was odd, but it felt good so I didn't stop him. My cock was so hard, straining against my black briefs, desperate to get out and be touched. Beau stared up at me for a few seconds, before turning his undivided attention to my cock. His mouth moved over my bulge through the cotton material, the heat of his mouth still finding its way through. His tongue slid over the head, his teeth nipping down the underside gently as I felt my knees go weak. I found my voice, even if it did come out a bit shaky.

"That feels so good, Beau."

He smiled at me and I put my hand in his soft hair, rumpling it even more. His fingers hooked in my waistband and started slowly pulling downward. My cock sprang free, hitting his lips and disappearing into his hot mouth in a split second.

The look in his eyes as he sucked the head of my cock made me gasp; the pure desire I saw there was overwhelming. I suddenly felt very sober and very clear as he swallowed my cock, rubbing my thighs as he sucked me hard. I held onto him with both hands but let him set the pace. I felt myself starting to slip, my orgasm getting too close, too fast. As if he read my mind, he let my cock leave his mouth and stood up.

He tackled me to the bed and we struggled together, wrestling for position, both of us laughing and trying to catch our breath. He was stronger than he looked and had no trouble pinning me on my stomach, his hands running a long line from my shoulders to my knees and back to my hips. Grabbing me roughly, he pulled my hips back until I was on my knees, my ass completely exposed to him. I felt a fingertip touch whisper over my asshole, moving in tiny circles around my rim. His words were so simple, but they cut through me like a knife. It was the question I was waiting for him to ask.

"I really want to fuck you, Scott. Would that be all right?"

"Yes. God, yes. Fuck me."

He let me up, and I dug in my nightstand drawers to find the condoms and lube we needed. Beau took them from me, kissing me softly all over my face, dragging me back down onto the bed. Lying next to me, he opened the lube and poured, rubbing his hands together slowly. One hand grasped my aching cock and the other went back to my puckered hole. His moist fingers plied me and opened me up. His lips stayed on mine, my hands groping at him, where ever I could reach.

"Are you ready for me, Scott?"

"Yeah. I'm ready."

He released me and rolled on the condom quickly, spooning behind me, his breathing quick and warm on my neck. I turned and looked at him, keeping my eyes locked to his as the head of his cock pushed slowly inside me. His hand rubbed down my back, urging me to relax as he moved deeper, inch by inch. When I felt his pubes tickle against me, I knew he was in to the hilt. My hand jerked my cock, trying to keep time with his thrusting hips.

"Scott, you feel so good."

I wanted to respond, but I couldn't. His words hit like lightning, turning my stomach upside down. He fucked me slowly, then quickly, his pace uneven and maddening. He grabbed my neck and pulled me into a deep kiss, breaking our gaze for the first time since we started. I nuzzled against his neck, enticed by the smell of him, every little thing about him fueling my fire. Beau pinched one of my nipples, sending a zip of pain and pleasure straight to my balls. I knew I couldn't hold out much longer; he was just too much.

"Beau, I'm really close. I'm gonna cum."

"Me too. cum for me, Scott. I want to watch you."

My cock twitched in my hand, my fist not even making it back to the base before I was cumming, shooting all over my stomach. I cried out, but most of it got lost in his mouth, his kisses swallowing up the sound. It was seconds later that he shot, pounding into me just a little bit harder. I was sweaty and drained as he pulled out of me, dropping down next to me on the bed. We cleaned up, and I watched him move to pick up his clothes. I wanted to stop him, but I was suddenly so tired, I could barely sit up. I managed to grasp his hand and stop him momentarily.

"Hey. Don't go. You can stay the night if you want to."

His smile was crippling, and when he kissed me, I felt another rush of warmth hit my body.

"Can't stay. I've gotta get the truck back. It was great, Scott. Really amazing."

I tried to pull him back again, to stop him, but he was still to strong for me.

"Don't leave, Beau. Please."

I didn't want to sound desperate, but I was overtaken with the feeling I would never see him again. He smiled, but I could tell I wasn't going to get him to stay.

"My name's not Beau. That isn't my shirt. I was just filling in for a friend of mine. I'm not the usual tow truck driver. You sure made my crappy night a whole lot better. But I really have to go."

Alcohol was still messing with my brain and I struggled to understand him. He got to the door and I called out to him.

"Wait, what do you mean your name isn't Beau? Then, who are you?"

"I'm the Prince of Tires."

I woke up to the sounds of a ringing phone, my head pounding with each noise. I ignored the call and tried to figure out what the hell had happened after Stacy and Rob's party. Most of the details were fuzzy, but I remembered all the important things. Everything about Beau was as clear as day. I knew the name didn't suit him, but I never imagined he would be someone else completely.

The fact that I didn't know his name was driving me crazy. The phone rang again, but once again, I let my voicemail take it. I got up and saw evidence of the previous evening all over the house. The condom was in the trash and my clothes still lay in the hall where I dropped them.

When I looked in the mirror before my shower, I saw a small mark on my neck, and my mind went back to Beau and his teeth scraping over my skin. The memory sent a cramp through my guts, the whole scene burned onto my mind as if it was branded there.

I couldn't get him out of my head all weekend long. Every time I stopped moving for a second, Beau was back in the front of my mind. I was distracted at work on Monday, and even more distracted at home. I could still smell him on my sheets, and still feel his hands on my hips if I closed my eyes. Trying to ignore the distraction, I convinced myself it was just a great one-night stand, and nothing more. But by the time Thursday rolled around, I was restless and knew I had to see Beau again, if only to confirm he existed and wasn't just some fantasy I had drunk to life. I decided to take a sick day on Friday and start searching.

The last words Beau said to me rang through my head. I wondered what the fuck "Prince of Tires" meant and how I might find him again. I didn't have the number of the tow truck company and I couldn't for the life of me remember what the side of the truck said. The shirt he wore didn't have a company name on it, and when I opened the phone book, I couldn't believe how many garages and tire shops there were in my town. Since I didn't know who to ask for, calling seemed like a waste of time. I grabbed the phone book and my keys and went out to search for my prince.

In each auto parts store, tire shop, lube station, and garage, I asked the same series of questions. None of them had a tow truck driver named Beau. And not one of them had ever heard of the Prince of Tires. Some laughed at my inquiries, but most just looked at me as if I was crazy. With each address in the phone book, I was getting less and less hopeful of ever finding him. Maybe he worked out of town, or maybe he told me some line of shit because he didn't want to see me again. I turned the page of the phone book and realized I was down to my last three chances. After strike one and two, I was all out of hope.

As I pulled into Zalinski's garage and turned off the car, my heart sank. The place didn't look very promising, and I didn't see any tow trucks parked by the building. I pushed open the door, and a loud bell announced my arrival. The girl behind the counter barely looked up, popping her gum as I walked toward her. I cleared my throat and she finally made eye contact but didn't say a word. I didn't wait for pleasantries and just jumped right into my crazy questions.

"Hi. This might sound like a weird question, but does a guy named Beau work here? He's a tow truck driver."

She stared at me blankly, her thick black eyeliner making her look kind of scary. I waited a few seconds, hoping that she would at least give me an answer. A puff of air came out of her mouth and made her bangs fly up.

"You're right, that is kind of a weird question. Nope. Nobody named Beau works here."

"Thanks anyway."

I turned to walk out, my last hope dashed as I opened the door. Before I could step outside, the girl called after me.

"Wait, hold on a second. There was guy who quit a few weeks ago whose name was Beau. He drove sometimes, but he really only got hired because he was a friend of Joey's. I guess it pays to be the prince, sometimes."

My eyes widened at her words and I ran back to the counter. I knew I must have misheard her, but I had to be sure.

"Did you say the prince?"

"Yeah, that's what they call Joey. You know, since his dad is the king."

She said it like it was the most obvious thing in the world, but I still didn't get it. Now, she was looking at me like I was a moron, as if her answer was the most obvious thing in the world.

"You know, Jake Zalinski, the King of Tires? That's our slogan."

My brain clicked in and I realized I was in the right place. I couldn't hide my smile, which made my new friend behind the counter look nervous.

"Is Joey here? I really need to talk to him."

"Why didn't you just say that from the beginning? He's upstairs. Through the door, first office on the left."

"Thanks. Really, you have no idea."

I left her puzzled and ran up the stairs, my palms sweaty and clammy. When I got to the door she specified, I froze. I worried that I had done all this for nothing, and that he really didn't want me to find him. Despite all my fears, I knocked lightly on the door, and heard his familiar voice telling me to come in.

I pushed open the door slowly and saw him sitting behind a messy desk. He looked up and saw me, and I braced for the worst. He sat back and started laughing, and I felt like someone had punched me in the stomach. It wasn't the reaction I had hoped for. I started backing away, but his words stopped me in my tracks.

"Wait, don't go."

My fear melted away as he smiled again, motioning me to the chair by the wall.

"So, you figured it out, I see. Took you long enough."

"Well, you didn't make it easy on me. Come on, Zalinski was the very last listing in the phonebook. You could have given me more to go on."

"Sorry, Scott. I know I should have just told you, but I have to be honest, I wasn't so sure I wanted to be found at first. But I couldn't stop thinking about you and about the other night. I was going to look you up and call today, but it looks like you beat me to the punch."

I relaxed, feeling my breathing return to normal. His hands opened and closed, and he looked nervous as he leaned forward a bit, smiling at his admission. I put my hand on his desk and fiddled with a paperweight shaped like a hubcap. I tried to look at him, but I was suddenly feeling timid.

"So, it's Joey? It suits you better than Beau."

"Yup, I'm Joey, Prince of Tires. I do the books, and know nothing about tires and very little about cars. My dad is so proud."

"I'm sure he is. After all, you're going to rule all this someday."

"And what a kingdom it is, Scott."

He laughed again, rubbing a hand through his hair. God, he was even cuter when my head was clear. He reached out across his desk and put his hand on mine. Our fingers laced together, and I felt the warmth of his hand all over my body. He pulled me forward, forcing me to stand up, and kissed me. The taste of him took me right back to that crazy night.

"So, Joey. What do we do now? How is this going to work?"

He shot me a sly smile, one that I knew I would fall in love with.

"Haven't you read your fairy tales, Counselor? Once you find your prince, you get to live happily ever after."

"Maybe we could try a date first, see how it goes."

"I don't remember that being in any of the old stories, Scott."

"It's not. It's in ours."

RECKLESS

Janine Ashbless

When the boar breaks from the thicket and charges straight at Alberic's back, I have no time to ground the butt of my boar spear properly or even to shout a warning. I simply shoulder-barge the prince aside and stand in the animal's path, aiming the spear point as best I can. For a moment my whole world fills up with the boar's black bristling head and its foaming chops; then the beast strikes me full-on. I'm knocked off my feet and dragged, flailing. I'm battered by kicking trotters before my head whacks up against the base of a sapling. Then the boar wrenches its tusks free of my padded jerkin and flees—taking my spear with it, buried to the cross-guard in its shoulder. The demonic squeal of the beast is overlaid with the baying of the hounds and the shouts of men running after.

As I lie there winded, with my mouth full of leaf mould and the seep of blood, the strangest picture flashes through my mind: a memory from when I was twelve and Alberic was seven, soon after my appointment. The prince had stolen a venison pie from the kitchen, but I was taking the whipping for it. Vividly the tow-headed boy's expression comes back before my inner eye: at first incredulous relief and then, twisting, tears. *Don't! Don't hit Tancred!* he wept. *It wasn't him!* The steward who'd been invested with the task of punishment paused briefly in his labors and let the leather strap hang slack. *Let this be a lesson to you, my lord: when you misbehave, others suffer for it. There are always consequences to your actions.*

I am lucky, aren't I, that he was a warm-hearted child and not a vindictive one? My childhood could have been an antechamber of hell otherwise. As it happened, we were well suited to friendship. *Look at the two of them*, they said at court. *Aren't they a handsome pair of youths? One fair and one dark, but like brothers.*

The king himself had told me, *The Dark must uphold the Light, Tancred. You must see that he grows up a fine man and a fine prince. You must protect him with your life and care for him with all your heart.*

They will never know the pain that has caused me. More than the steward ever inflicted, certainly.

My first actions, when I can breathe again, are to cough out the forest litter from my mouth and thrust my hand through the rent in my jerkin to my aching belly. To my intense relief I find the leather and the quilted layers of linen torn, but no hot ooze of blood from my stomach. By now the forest has stopped heaving around me like a stormy sea, and as I try to raise myself to my elbow I see Alberic bending over me, concern on his face.

"Tancred! Are you hurt?"

With a rush I'm overwhelmed once more by a vision of the boar: red-rimmed eyes and yellow tusks, the hot stink of its breath.

"I'm whole, Sire." The blood in my mouth is only from my split lip. Nothing fit to complain about.

The scream and the foul reek of the boar stay in my head though, as hands clap me on the back and men drag me to my feet. It stays even as we run on through the wood, following the sound of the hounds and their quarry, now at battle. Only when the kill is done and we've retrieved our horses and are riding back to the hunting lodge with the carcass of the huge boar slung from a pole, do I begin to feel my normal self—just as my many bruises and my wrenched joints begin to complain.

Our success at the hunt is the occasion of celebration. The ladies who've waited all day at their pavilion in the meadow are greatly impressed by the size of the boar and praise Prince Alberic for his courage in striking the final blow. They garland us all with summer wildflowers. The other courtiers involved in the chase slap me on the back and roar with laughter as they recount the details, delighted by the way I've pulled the beard of Death. Servants scurry about pouring wine, and I take a deep draught that makes my head spin anew. I'm not nearly as amused by the day's events as others are; I just want to sit down and have something decent to eat and for Lord Drufus to stop braying in my ear. Eventually the prince notices my bleak expression and holds up his hand for silence.

"Listen, listen," he calls, beckoning everyone into a circle with his goblet. The courtiers gather expectantly. Alberic is well liked: pleasant and open-handed, he knows how to win hearts. Bold in his hunting and merry in his dancing, when prompted he can turn his mind to the more serious affairs of state, and he will make a fine king someday. And the fact that he is so hand-some does not diminish his popularity with the people at all; with his sandy blond hair and blue eyes and straight figure, he is the very image of a young prince. He can barely set foot out of doors without being surrounded by a mob of flirtatious young women.

"Let me tell you all," says Alberic, laying his hand on my shoulder, "the value of a good counselor." The faces around us are expectant and smiling. "When we went out to the hunt and the boar took cover in the thicket, my dark raven here warned me that we should stay on horseback and not pursue on foot. I took no notice of his wise words."

There's a hum of laughter in the little crowd. Ordinarily I would not care: I'm used to playing the foil to the prince's golden glamour. Although only five years the elder, it's my allotted role to rein in Alberic's more reckless impulses and to teach him to think before he acts, as well as to guard his life. Sober when the prince is playful, the dour and vigilant Tancred—oh, I know my reputation, and normally it doesn't bother me one whit. I'm the only man here who can beat Alberic at swordplay, which mollifies my pride. But today I feel a burn of irritation at the crowd's amusement. What do they know about it—those vacuous ladies in their silken dresses so inappropriate for the forest, and those blustering toadying men so desperate for the prince's favor? What do they know about guarding a life so precious that I must be prepared to offer up my own if necessary?

"Then he told me that if I must continue on foot that I should use the spear instead of my sword. And I didn't take that advice either, because I thought, *What would a royal prince look like, using a spear like an ordinary huntsman?*"

Another buzz of amusement. Alberic puts his arm around my shoulders. Years of practice come to my aid: I do not let the inner quiver of my muscles translate to a visible reaction.

"Then the boar came out at me as if from nowhere. I had my back to it. And it would have gutted me like a fish, except that this man threw himself in the way. He saved my life!"

A rising murmur, but a respectful one. I tongue the inside of my swollen lip, exploring the edges of the torn flesh.

"Let me ask you: What greater service to a prince can there be than that? What finer loyalty? Tancred, kneel down."

A little stiffly, for my right knee is throbbing, I kneel. Alberic draws off a ring from his hand and signals for me to raise my own. The emerald catches the light, greener than the grass about us, as he slides the ring over my thumb. "Let all witness my gratitude to this man, Lord Tancred. Let everyone know that I have no truer champion and no greater friend." Stooping, he takes my face in his hands and kisses my forehead: a royal blessing.

Our audience applauds, and as I rise to my feet again they cheer me. It isn't my place to make a speech in return, but I meet Alberic's eyes and nod, a private flash of acknowledgment passing between us.

But still I can't smile.

Soon afterward we repair to the lodge to change out of our sweaty hunting clothes and dress for the dinner that will be laid out in the pavilion. Servants bring linen cloths and bowls of hot water to the prince's chamber and kneel to tug off our high-topped boots, then retire as we strip off our vambraces and padded jerkins. Alberic flings his crown of may-blossom over a wall-mounted rack of antlers with a laugh and is soon talking away happily, but I do little more than grunt.

This is always a part of the day that I dread as much as anticipate, and today in particular I cannot shake off the black cloud over my shoulders. As the prince's companion, I usually share his bedchamber—or his tent when on campaign, or his carriage. On one shamefully arousing occasion I even shared his bed and the lady-in-waiting in it; afterward her story, whispered in confidence to friends, became the envy of the court. Understand: we do not seek privacy from one another.

This rustic room in the hunting lodge is no different. Its high windows let in shafts of dusty light, and I covertly watch Alberic make the motes roil as he crosses the beams. The prince's hair is standing up in sweaty tufts, and the golden dusty light clings to that too, and to the smooth and glistening skin of his shoulders as he washes his chest. Little dark flecks of forest debris are plastered across his back; I ache to brush them off. Alberic has no upper-body hair except for the sun-blonded streaks on the backs of his forearms; the muscles of his hard stomach are as smooth as ripples in sand, and as golden. It's one of the many images that haunt me at night.

Water droplets lick the furrows of his ribs under his raised arm and race to darken the upper edge of his hose. The sight makes my stones grow heavy in their tightening purse of skin. It's always like this: he's oblivious and I am in torment.

With an effort, I pull off my torn shirt and glance down at my own torso. Like the prince's, my body is honed by fencing and hunting and hard riding. The bruises won't show up properly until tomorrow, but there's a pink furrow scored across the flat of my stomach, slicing through the dark hair, almost all the way down to where my hose sits low on my hips.

"What's that?" Alberic asks.

"That's where the boar's tusk grazed me."

Alberic swears a mild oath and crosses over to touch the scraped skin with his wet fingertips. His touch tickles and I have to force myself to hold still. The smell of Alberic's fresh hot sweat is pushing through his cologne and my cock jerks in response to the touch and the scent, making me nervous. "Another inch closer and..." says the prince, wonderingly.

"And I'd have been disemboweled." I can feel myself quivering, and to mask the tremble I brush Alberic's fingers away.

"You're angry at me?"

"Yes." It's a relief to admit it.

"Because I risked your life?" The cheeriness dies out of Alberic's expression. "I'm sorry; you know that. I got carried away in the excitement. It was a bit reckless, I know."

"Yes it was." In private, we dispense with formal politeness. "But I'm not angry because I was at risk—I'm angry because you were."

"Me?" The smile flashes into Alberic's eyes again. "You worry too much, Tancred. Cluck cluck cluck, like a hen."

"It's my job to keep you alive."

"Oh, we can't have me dying and making you looking bad, can we?"

Anger flares in my breast. "Can you not take it seriously? If not for my sake, then your father's?"

"My father?"

"Do you want to break his heart one day? And what do you think he'll do if his only son gets himself killed or maimed? Do you think he's going to produce another heir with a snap of his fingers?"

"There's always my sister...."

"Alberic, be serious. You're the heir to the throne. For twenty-three years you've been prepared for your role. You have a responsibility to all of us."

The prince just grins. "Stop being sulky, Tancred." He clasps my face firmly, framing it in his hands, looking me in the eyes. "I know how much you've done for me. I haven't forgotten. I appreciate every bit." Then he swoops in and plants a kiss on my lips. It's a firm, quick, masculine kiss—a prince's benison. The sort of intimacy only royalty gives one the right to bestow.

Once more I hear the thunder of the boar's feet.

I react without thinking, just as in the woods. Reaching round, my hand grips the back of Alberic's neck, holding him so that he can't pull away. My mouth seizes his. Angrily. Needfully. For a moment I know nothing but his lips, his tongue, the taste of the wine he's been drinking, the taint of my own blood. For a moment he does not react. Then he tries to pull back—and I hold him, refusing to let him go. I am too hungry for his mouth.

I don't know why I do it this time, when never before. It just happens.

Eventually he pushes me hard in the chest and we break with a gasp.

"What was that?" His voice is a hoarse whisper.

God have mercy on me, I say to myself, my eyes suddenly opened to my actions. What had I been thinking of? I'm as shocked as he is, but unlike Alberic I'm stunned into a kind of resignation. My voice sounds unfamiliar as I say the unsayable. "That was love, Sire."

"What?"

I'm going to be exiled. I'll never see him again. Terror makes me dizzy. My brown eyes meet his wide blue ones. "I love you."

"Of course you do—I'm your prince!"

"No, Alberic."

There's a rising note in his voice. "As a brother to me, then!"

I shake my head. "No."

The blow takes me by surprise: back-handed across the face and hard enough to stagger me. I put my hand up to my cheek. *He's in a panic*, I tell myself. *He has no idea how to react to such a shock. I have always been like his elder brother.*

"Get on your knees, vassal!"

I obey. I feel sick, the conflicting instincts tearing at each other inside me. I half-expect Alberic to strike me again, but he throws up his hands instead.

"This is a joke, isn't it? A sick joke!" My one blessing is

that Alberic isn't shouting: his voice is raspy with strain but kept deliberately quiet. If he does start shouting at me, there are plenty of people within earshot who will hear everything.

"No joke, Sire."

"But I've seen you! With women!"

"Women are," I shrug, unable to say out loud, *I did what was expected of me*, "all very well. But it's you alone that I love."

"You want to *fuck* me?"

I don't answer. I want to fuck him. I want to wrap him in my arms and feel his hot hard muscles contesting mine. I want to be inside him and him to be in me. I want to feel his strength and his eagerness and his appetite. I want to taste him: his spunk and his sweat, his tears and his kisses. Wanting to fuck him isn't even the half of it.

I cannot say that. I don't have to. He reads it in my eyes.

"How dare you?" I'd never seen Alberic look so distressed. The blood has risen in an unbecoming flush to his face. "How...?" he chokes. "You want to play the woman for me, do you?" He fumbles at his insulted crotch. "You want this, do you? You like it?" Unlacing his hose, he pulls out the member in question. "Then suck my cock. Kneel there and take it."

It's half-hard, I see, and my heart wallops painfully against the inside of my breastbone. If he thinks he's humiliating me then he has misjudged badly. I've fantasized about his cock for years. I've seen it when he's undressed, when we swim together, when he makes water. I've seen it shriveled with chill, and all perky of a morning, and long and silky and relaxed when he stretches his body out after exercising. He's never attempted to hide it; indeed sometimes I think he is flaunting it. His prick is almost as familiar to me as my own, and an imagined accompaniment to my every erection. How can I recoil now, when there are nights I've lain in my bed and tasted my own semen on my fingers and pretended it was Alberic's?

"There." He's nearly crying. "That's what you want, isn't it?" And he shoves it into my face and thrusts it into my unresisting mouth. Soft skin; thick meat wrapped in satin. It is my first. Strange to think that I've never had a man in my mouth before; I've never dared risk the public shame, the destruction of my life at his side.

It tastes unfamiliar—musky, sweaty, faintly pissy—and yet my mouth fastens upon it with instinctive appetite. And though it's easily manageable at first, so that I can engulf the whole thing and lap at his scrotum with my tongue, it doesn't stay that way. In moments it's thickening, lengthening, hardening. I have to move back as it fills my mouth and nudges into my throat.

Merciful God, but it excites me. Every thrust of his makes my own cock jump and swell. I grab at myself through the cloth of my hose, knowing that I have an inexcusable hard-on already, should he look down. Can he tell how eager my sucking is, how grateful? That the tears he has forced to my eyes are not simply testament to how he is choking me with his polearm?

Alberic gasps my name. His spread hands frame his crotch as he thrusts clumsily into my mouth. He's hard now, really hard: his weapon set and braced like a boar spear. I get one hand on his cock just to gain myself breathing space, and he freezes. My tongue traces the slit of his glans, tasting a slippery ooze there, exploring the tiny wrinkled delta of his frenulum until he moans in his chest. The noise is half-protest, half-plea.

It is a signal that changes everything.

I rise to my feet, his shaft still gripped in my fingers. We are matched in height as well as in physique, so we lock gazes eye to eye. There is no anger in him any more: I've sucked it all out of him and taken it for my own. There is only fear in his wide eyes, and need. I can still taste his cock on my bruised lips. It's intoxicating. I give his prick a little tug, caressing the ball of my thumb across his slippery glans. The tilt of his hips tells me all I need to know. The emerald on the ring he's gifted me gleams.

"You don't want me to stop, do you?" I whisper.

Alberic's jaw works as he tries to swallow. He can't answer. He can't move. I've got a hold of his erect cock and he's my captive, caught on the cusp of surrender and the brink of admitting the unthinkable. With my free hand I tug roughly at the laces of his clothing to expose him more. I want to see his balls; they are fat and tight, the scrotum nearly hairless. A golden pomegranate, bursting with seed—*how very unlike my own darkly haloed purse of stones,* I think as I cup them, giving them a slow, loving squeeze.

Then I hold him in place as I unlace my hose and release my own cock, and we both watch as my shaft springs up to meet his. They're angled like crossed foils at the start of a duel—and matched, once more: each weapon as thickly erect as the other. Deliberately I butt and rub my shaft against his, and Alberic's intake of breath is harsh.

My cock on his cock. I have waited so long for this. Mine is so hard I could hammer horseshoes on it.

I don't spare him. Taking both pricks between my palms I press them together, rubbing up against him. His eyes are bright with fear but his lips are parted and eager, and there is no flagging of the hot stiff meat in my hands.

"Tancred," he gasps.

He has no idea that his shock is the mirror of my own. Every muscle in my body is quivering. The difference between us is simply that I know what I want. I push him backward, using his stiff cock like a handle, until the back of his legs meet the edge of his bed and fold. I push him down upon the coverlet and straddle him. My joints protest: I barely noticed. Then I take up his hand

and lick his palm and fingers and press them into service, holding
both our shafts one against the other. My hand assists too from
the other side, so we are both holding, both straining.

"Kiss me," I whisper, stooping over him, moving on him.
Alberic's lips part and I cover them with my mouth, sinking into
his kiss. His tongue tangles with mine. Stubble rasps stubble.
Ball-sacs squash together. Cock slides and rubs over cock within
the interlaced cage of our fingers.

I taste his breath as he groans into my mouth. I'm moving on
him, trying not to be too clumsy, too jagged, despite my inexpe-
rience. Our limbs are a knot. His fingers dig into my thigh. I can
feel the perspiration moistening our skins as we slither together.
His kiss is hot and breathy. And then all of a sudden it's a wild
gasping muddle of lips and cheeks and panted blasphemies as he
comes to crisis, his jism spurting over and slicking the head of
my cock. Like a pine knot pressed to one already ablaze, I too
catch fire and my spend gushes forth over him, mingling with his
own. Spasm after spasm racks us both until I collapse, groaning,
and slide off him.

The world spins, and when it settles north is no longer north
and south no longer south.

"Holy Mother of Christ," gasps Alberic, looking down at
himself.

There is semen splashed all over his heaving, sweat-slick
chest and belly, and no telling to which of us any of it belongs.
Our seed is inextricably mingled, and I mingle it further as I rake
my fingertips through it and stroke his fallen weapon. Softening
now, that cock still throbs with life. But I'm not looking at it; my
attention is all on Alberic's face, awaiting his edict even as we
each try to regain control of our panting breath.

I might have a hold of his cock, but my prince holds my life
in his hands.

"Is that what you call love, then?" he asks at length.

I have the grace to feel ashamed. "Sire...I..."

"Tancred." A grin blossoms on Alberic's face and he begins to laugh. But there are still strains of nervousness in there. "Fuck, Tancred." The laughter dies suddenly, leaving his blue eyes dark and vertiginously deep. Then he kneels up on the bed. That golden light plays across the pearlescent glisten on his torso.

I don't move, except to lie back. I want to see him, all of him, no matter what he's going to say next, no matter how he's going to punish me. I want to fix that beauty in my mind.

"I don't know what to ..." He shakes his head. "Tancred. For heaven's sake. What do I do?"

"I don't know."

"You're my advisor. Tell me."

I draw a deep breath. My heartbeat, which has been slowing, picks up. I raise myself on my elbows. "Take my cock in your mouth."

Alberic's eyes widen. "You think?" he manages to ask, after a moment's hesitation.

"I do," I say solemnly, and then—as Alberic slides down and bows his head over my lap, his warm mouth opening over my already resurgent cock—add, "Sire."

THE FROG PRINCE

Josephine Myles

So? Simon? Are you going to be helping out or not?" Lizzie asked, the seeming innocence of her question belied by the arch smile she gave me.

I thrust the spade down into the soil and straightened, attempting to stretch all the aches out of my back. "I don't know. Scooping up frogs and toads doesn't really sound like my kind of thing." I neglected to mention how I'd nearly chopped my foot in half when a frog had startled me by hopping into my trench earlier. The idea of having to handle them, even with gloves on, made me shudder.

"Jasper specifically asked if you'd be coming." It was true, but it had been in front of the whole group and certainly didn't merit the significance Lizzie seemed determined to invest it with.

"He just wants extra bodies. It's not like he's asking me on a date or anything."

"He was flirting with you." Lizzie was in full matchmaker mode, that glint in her eye giving her away like it always did.

"Jasper flirts with everyone. It doesn't mean anything." I glanced over to where Jasper had his sleeves rolled up and was tutoring the older volunteers in the best way to set up a protective tunnel of horticultural fleece over the seeds we had all just planted. His hair shone like a golden halo in the weak March sunshine, and the rich rumble of his laughter tickled my eardrums despite the distance.

It was as if the earth had thrown forth an early sunflower— no, scratch that—Jasper wasn't a plant. His vitality and constant motion most definitely put him in the animal kingdom. He was the sole reason I had caved in to Lizzie's persistent demands that I join her in volunteering at Henley's new organic allotment project, and he was the one thing that kept me coming, the memories of his smiles helping me ignore the aches and pains that haunted me every Monday.

Such a shame the guy was straight; not that a charismatic looker like Jasper Fitzroy would be interested in an ordinary bloke like me, anyway. I watched Celia Huntingdon lay a possessive hand on his bronzed forearm and caught the flash of his teeth magnified by the cool, clear air.

"Just give it up, Lizzie. He's definitely straight."

"Yeah, right." Lizzie gave me a pitying look, and I contemplated whether my life would be worth living if I pushed her over into the manure heap. "You just keep telling yourself that, Simon Goodchild, and then you'll never have to risk making a move, will you?"

"It's not like that," I muttered, resuming my double digging with a vigor that made my muscles scream. That was the problem with childhood friends. They could always see right through you.

* * *

It was Monday morning, and I was on my hands and knees in Goodchild's, the last remaining independent bookstore in Henley-on-Thames, a town most people know only for its annual rowing races. My aching muscles were hampering my efforts to adjust the height of a low shelf to accommodate some belligerently oversized art books, when an unexpected "Hey there" sent my head into collision with the shelf above.

I slumped on the floor, my hand absently rubbing the crown of my head as my eyes panned up the intruder's muddy boots, long, khaki-clad legs and perfectly fitted tweed jacket to find Jasper's apologetic face crowning off the ensemble. He held out a hand to help pull me up.

"Sorry about that, Simon. Didn't mean to give you a fright." He was still holding onto my hand, which had broken out in a cold sweat as if to make up for the fact that my mouth was as dry as a stale sponge cake. "Nice place you have here. Is it yours?"

"Yes, I inherited it from my uncle. The shop and the flat upstairs." I yanked my hand free, wiping it on my trousers then flushing as I realized how rude that might have appeared. Fortunately Jasper didn't seem to mind. He was still gazing at me with amusement twitching at his lips. The sun and wind had colored his face, bestowing a sprinkling of freckles across the bridge of his nose and a glow to his cheeks, which further highlighted the warm tones of his eyes. The March drizzle hadn't flattened his tousled hair like it would mine; instead, it had crowned him with glittering droplets that clung on to the golden locks. It wasn't fair. All the great outdoors seemed to have done for me was to chap my lips and give a ruddy cast to my nose, making me look more like I'd been going overboard on the brandy rather than toiling in the fresh air.

"Are you looking for anything in particular?" I managed to croak, gesturing around my kingdom as my bookseller's persona re-formed around me like a protective shell. I pointed to my newly stocked gardening shelf. "I've ordered in a few interesting organic gardening books after hearing you talk. There's one on companion planting."

God, I sounded like a teacher's pet now, bringing in prized possessions to impress my idol. I had to clamp my mouth shut to prevent myself blathering on about my motley collection of houseplants: a scruffy spider plant, a leggy money tree, and a shriveled-up cactus that I was beginning to suspect was in fact dead. God forbid he would ever get to find out what a fraud I was—feigning an interest in gardening when all I really wanted was a few more minutes basking in his presence.

"Actually, Simon, I was looking for you." Jasper's warm voice wrapped around me, his amber eyes dancing with suggestive connotations, making me lightheaded as my blood started to move south.

"Oh!"

"Yes, I wanted to make sure that you'll be coming along to help with the frog patrol tonight. You didn't give me a definite answer yesterday."

"Oh." Of course. Bloody frogs. "Yes. I'd love to help." I smiled weakly, hoping that my mind's stubborn insistence on imagining Jasper fucking me on the shop floor wasn't visible in my eyes.

After he left, I was so wound up that I couldn't concentrate on restocking the art shelves any more. I kept seeing that light in Jasper's eyes that seemed to promise so much. In the end, I had to flip the "Back in ten minutes" sign on the door and take myself up to my bed in order to calm down. With Jasper in mind, it didn't take long.

* * *

"Right, so we'll have teams of two people per bucket and spade, and the team who collects the most wins a round of drinks from the losers. Sound fair, folks?" Jasper swung his torch around the loose circle of assembled volunteers, and there were some chuckles and a few "Hear, hears."

"Okay then, let's help these little fellas get to their party in one piece." Jasper sounded so hearty, I wondered how anyone could feel such enthusiasm about saving a few lowly amphibians from death by car tire. Still, here I was, the green phony seduced into helping save the planet by a hopeless crush.

I could feel my heart thumping as I waited to see if Jasper would come over, but when Mrs. Templeton pounced on him I turned to Lizzie with a sigh. "Looks like you were wrong, *again*."

Lizzie scowled, throwing the spade at me. "Right then, Mister, you'd better make yourself useful and start shoveling."

The sky had cleared over the afternoon, the only reminders of the morning's rain the ragged clouds scudding high overhead and the glistening droplets covering every leaf and stem, shining like jewels in the torchlight. We worked along our twenty-meter stretch of the road, Lizzie holding the torch and bucket while I scooped up any frogs and toads that seemed to be headed in the right direction.

It wasn't so bad with a spade's length between my hands and the creatures, and after a while I started to get cocky, flipping them into the bucket with a flourish that they didn't appreciate, if the disgruntled croaks were anything to go by. When the mass of amphibians reached a critical level, we ferried them across the road and dumped them unceremoniously over the gate to the allotments, leaving them to find their own way to the pond.

Leaning on the gate and staring down at the heap of writhing frogs in the circle of torchlight, I felt a hand clap heavily onto my shoulder.

"Magnificent sight, isn't it? All those horny males, just desperate to mate." Jasper's voice was low and intimate, and I noticed out of the corner of my eye that Lizzie was making off with the bucket and spade, grinning as she abandoned me. "The males wake from hibernation first, and get so excited that they'll hump anything remotely frog-shaped. Even fish, sometimes." I looked up in surprise. "Oh yes, what you're witnessing down there is an all-male frog orgy."

I gulped, glanced down at the pile of gay frogs and back up into Jasper's eyes. He winked at me, knelt, and for one delirious moment I imagined him mouthing me through my jeans, but then he thrust a hand through the gate and stood up with a pair of frogs in his hands. I shone the torch on them. Was it wrong to feel so turned on while watching a pair of male frogs humping?

"They develop these dark swellings on their forefingers to help them grip on to their mate."

Jasper showed me the way the bottom frog's fingers kept the top frog well and truly welded to him. I couldn't help but notice the calluses on Jasper's own hands, and before my mind could leap in and stop me I ran a fingertip over the one on his thumb. The thought of him gripping my hips with those roughened pads of skin made my cock leap to attention. I closed my eyes, swallowing, and when I opened them he was staring at me with a question in his gold-flecked eyes. *The same color as the frogs' eyes,* my dazed mind helpfully supplied.

I licked my lips, desperate to get some moisture back onto them so that I could form a sentence, although I had no idea what I would say. I had to say something though, or he was going to think I was well and truly inarticulate. "Is it true that you can lick toads to get high?"

I wanted to kick myself for asking such a moronic question. I didn't want Jasper to think that I was some kind of hippie wannabe; not that he was likely to think that, given my sensible clothes and responsible occupation. That and the fact that I lived in Henley, a town so middle England that you could smell the waxed Mercedes and hampers full of strawberries, cream, and champagne every fine summer's day.

Jasper seemed interested, though, his eyes twinkling in the torchlight. "There are certain species of toad in the Americas that have psychoactive compounds in their venom, but you would have to milk their venom glands to get enough of the stuff. The licking story is an urban legend, I'm afraid." The pink tip of Jasper's tongue flicked out, the gesture deliberate and downright dirty. I could imagine that tongue doing wicked things to me.

"Frogs have very long tongues." Oh great, now I really sounded like a monosyllabic imbecile, wittering on about frogs, my voice thick with lust.

"So do some humans," Jasper countered, and stuck his out to demonstrate, touching the tip of his nose with the glistening pink flesh. He raised his eyebrows in triumphant glee as I gasped.

"Wow!" I was beyond eloquence, all my finer words deserting me as my blood rushed south.

I dropped the torch. Jasper dropped the frogs. We were reaching blindly for each other when a light dazzled me.

"Hello there, chaps. Got us a bucketful of frogs here. I say, are we the first?"

"Not quite, Alan. I think Simon here's beaten you to it. He's a fast worker."

Muttering curses, I picked up the torch and stumbled in the direction I'd seen Lizzie take, Jasper's jovial response to our interrupter following me in the night air.

"Thank you so much for all your help, folks, but don't forget, there'll be more frogs tomorrow night. That's when the ladies should be emerging from their beauty sleep, so things will definitely heat up down in the pond." There was a chorus of tired chuckles from the assembled helpers.

A woman's voice called out, "Let's hear our appreciation for Jasper Fitzroy. Not only an inspirational teacher, but a true frog prince!" I joined in with the round of applause, pleased to see the blush stain Jasper's cheeks as he downplayed his role in events. But then he was swallowed up by a circle of well-wishers, and all I could see of him was his tousled hair sticking up above the ring of sleepy townsfolk.

I sighed and said my good-byes to Lizzie, then strolled back to the gate to add our bucket and spade to the pile. As I turned back toward home I felt that heavy, callused hand fall on my shoulder again.

"Wait, Simon. You promised you'd give me a hand getting all the equipment back in the shed, remember?"

I did? But when I saw the gleam in Jasper's eyes I knew that it wasn't just an illusion generated by the torchlight. He was looking at me like I was a fascinating species he wanted to save, and a surge of confidence revitalized my flirting gland, long since presumed atrophied—according to Lizzie, anyway.

"Are you saying you need a man to help sort out your equipment, Jasper?" Okay, it wasn't a great line, but I loaded it with as much suggestion as the words would carry and stood there, smirking at him as the smile spread over his whole face.

"That's right. Do you think you're man enough for the job? You certainly look like you are." I wanted to laugh as he gave me an appreciative once-over. It was so difficult to imagine what a man like that could possibly see in a lanky, mousy-haired bookworm like me. Yet clearly he did see something he liked, as my roving torch picked out a distinct swelling in the front of his trousers when it just happened to stray in that direction. Well!

We worked silently at stacking up the buckets, as if in agreement not to delay matters with pointless chit chat. When I had a chin-high pile of buckets in my arms, and Jasper had two armfuls of spades and shovels, we set off through the allotments toward the communal shed. There was just enough light from the crescent moon to spot the frogs on the crushed stone track, and I stepped carefully to avoid the stragglers.

Jasper strode on ahead of me, and I wished I had a hand free to train the torch on his backside, having to content myself with memories of how the pert cheeks stuck out as he hunkered down to demonstrate some gardening technique or intriguing minibeast. After we had stowed away the frog-saving kit, there was an awkward moment of standing in the shed, my dangling torch casting strange shadows on our faces, both unable to bridge the gap between us.

Jasper broke the silence. "I would invite you back to my place, but I'm lodging with a terribly nosy landlady and she's already told me that I'm not to bring anyone back after nine."

"Oh." I'd always imagined him as living in some little stone cottage, a verdant garden flourishing under his capable hands. I knew that I should be inviting him back to mine instead, but the words dried up in my mouth.

"Sit with me for a while." Jasper tugged at my hand and I let him lead me to the open doorway. We sat with our legs outside, looking out over the dark allotments. I could hear the frustrated calls of the frogs, but the way our thighs pressed together as we sat in the narrow doorway was claiming most of my attention. His heat permeated the cloth layers, and a rich, musky scent rose from his body, making me giddy with desire.

"So what brought you to Henley?" It was an innocuous question, but I felt on safer ground with small talk than resuming the flirting of earlier, and besides which, I really did want to know. I'd heard Jasper wax lyrical about soil, wildlife, fruit and vegetables, but I knew hardly anything about the man himself. He had a way of deflecting personal questions in front of the group, deftly changing the subject or sending the question back with a smile so disarming that his interlocutors didn't notice that they hadn't been answered.

I was surprised to hear a deep sigh.

"There were reasons I had to leave the last place I lived in. I made some stupid mistakes. Hurt people I cared about. But that's all over now."

I pondered this, but as Jasper was looking out over the allotment with his lips clamped tight, I figured he didn't want to share any more than that. His pain made me bold enough to offer comfort, though, and as I didn't have any words to respond to his cryptic statements, I reached out a hand and stroked his jaw. His stubble was rough under my bookseller's fingers, and as I held my hand there he rubbed against it in a feline gesture, a soft sound, half-gulp, half-sigh escaping his lips.

I lifted my hand to tangle it in his hair, turning his face toward me as I leant forward to catch his lips with mine. Jasper's mouth tasted sweet, like brandy, but it took a moment for him to start kissing me back. I began to pull away, worried that I'd made a mistake and read the signals wrong, but then he lunged for me with a startling ferocity. The scrape of his teeth against my lower lip, the insistent sweeping of his tongue and the warm bulk of his body pressing against me sent my thoughts careening away. Nothing mattered but this. This beautiful, charismatic man desiring me. Wanting me. Needing me.

Jasper's hands roamed possessively, and I retaliated, trying to map out every part of him with my fingers and palms. I searched for the warmth of his body under the layers of clothing, the hot, sweaty truth of him hidden under the tweedy armor. And when I ran my hands over the skin of his back he arched his spine, gasping, before falling on me again with renewed vigor, pushing us down onto the dusty boards inside the shed.

It felt like I was going to be smothered, and I sucked in air greedily as he moved down to my neck, tugging down on my jumper to reveal more flesh to ravish. His cock was digging into my hip, and I wanted nothing more than to taste him there; to have him thrust into my mouth and to know that it was me making him cum. Me making him shudder and groan and spill his seed.

With a strength I didn't know I had, I flipped us over, Jasper letting out a surprised-sounding chuckle as a pile of plastic seed trays toppled over next to us. With a growl I pushed over the second teetering stack before ripping open Jasper's shirt and starting work on his fly buttons. All finesse was abandoned in the desperate quest for more skin, although I did pause for a moment, helping Jasper to pull my jumper off. It fell over the torch, and for a moment all was panting, sweaty darkness, my heart pounding in my chest. The last button came free and his cock sprang up; I felt its heavy length in my hand as I freed him from his underpants.

But I needed to see him, to feast my eyes on Jasper, so I fumbled around for my jumper, my fingers clumsy with passion. I was distracted momentarily by his hands massaging my erection through my jeans. Then he moved on to deal with the zipper. When I finally located it, the torch rolled away, sending shadows racing across the shed, but I had enough light to take in Jasper spread beneath me, the skin of his sparsely haired chest flushed and damp with sweat, despite the cool of the night air. Oh, but he was gorgeous—his hair messed up by my fingers, his clothes torn open by my hands, his lips swollen by my kisses.

You are so fucking sexy, I thought.

But I must have said it out loud, because he gave me a smile, saying, "So are you." It was probably meaningless flattery, an instinctive polite response to my compliment, but it didn't feel like it when he was looking at me with that dark intensity. I shivered, whether from the cool of the air or some other stimulus I couldn't say, and bent down to press kisses to his chest and stomach, basking in the heat radiating from his skin.

Moving down, closer to my goal, I thrummed with excitement, with awe that this was finally happening. That I was about to be sucking on Jasper's cock like I'd been fantasizing about for months.

"Stop! Simon, wait, please."

I knew it was too good to be true. This was when I paid for my fantasies by having them all come crashing down around me. My stomach lurched and bile rose bitter in my throat.

But Jasper was smiling, his eyes still dark with lust.

"Move around, would you? I want to suck you at the same time."

As the relief washed over me I started to chuckle, and I managed to knock over yet another stack of plant pots in my haste to comply, feeling them roll against my back as I scrambled down on my side. But then the warmth of Jasper's breath against my cock wiped away all other thoughts, the touch of his tongue made me tremble with want, and if it hadn't been for his own cock nudging me in the face I don't think I'd have remembered that I was supposed to be reciprocating.

I took a moment to run my fingers over the velvety skin, burying my nose into his hair to draw in a lungful of his earthy musk, the scent driving me wild as I felt the heat of his lips enveloping me. As I licked him, relishing the flavor of his arousal and hearing Jasper's shuddering groan, I knew that neither of us would last long, but that it didn't matter.

Nothing mattered but the moist, sucking heat of his mouth around me, and the heavy press of his cock against my tongue, against the back of my throat as I drew him in deeper and deeper. Nothing mattered but the bucking of his hips and the gasping of his breath. Nothing mattered but the fact that we were here, doing this, together.

I came hard, cresting on a wave of sensation that crashed through me, barely aware of pulling back off Jasper and using my hand to pump him once, twice, my lips around the head of his cock to catch his semen and drink it down. Everything was perfect. The hard boards under me, the cool breeze against my exposed skin, the aftershocks that still wracked my body.

Jasper stood, turning away from me. I couldn't see his face, but the tension was written through his body and I closed my eyes to block the view. I should have known. This was too much to hope for. Too good to be true. This wasn't meant for me.

I stumbled to my feet, savagely wrenching my clothes back around me in an effort to halt the chill that was penetrating me to the core.

"Here, let me," Jasper whispered, and his hands came out to help me fasten my buttons. I wanted to push him away, because it felt too much like tenderness and I knew that it must be false, but my rebellious arms refused to cooperate with my mind, choosing to side with Jasper instead.

"Sit with me," Jasper said, so we sat back in the doorway, and the taste of his mouth was explained when he pulled a silver flask out of his pocket and the rich scent of brandy filled the air.

"It was my brother-in-law. Ralph." The words came from nowhere, but the deep undercurrents of feeling in his tone made me sit up and pay attention. I stayed silent while he took another swig from the flask before handing it to me.

"I fell for him the moment Topaz first brought him home for dinner. Watching them get married was torture, but then after Rupert was born, Ralph started seeking me out, saying he wanted to get away from all things baby related."

Jasper took a deep breath, and I looked up at his face, those lips now twisted with the bittersweet recollections. "He was just using me. I can see that now. But at the time I convinced myself that it was love, and when he started pulling away I couldn't cope and I made a scene in front of Topaz, and that's when everything came out."

Jasper closed his eyes, and I had to stifle the urge to kiss away the furrows on his brow. "When was this?" I asked, squeezing his hand gently.

"Last May. The family was in uproar. I was kicked off the estate. Oh yes," he said, catching my surprised expression. "I'm third in line to become the next Lord Freshford, believe it or not. I've never been bothered about the title, though; my brother's welcome to it. I was perfectly happy just being the estate manager. Leaving that land behind was the hardest thing I've ever had to do. Especially as Topaz let Ralph stay. Apparently it was all my fault, and I seduced him." He gave a harsh laugh. "Well, that might be true but he didn't put up much of a fight." The bitterness welled up in his voice, undercut with a depth of sorrow and what I thought must be self-reproach.

A surge of compassion overtook me, and I pulled Jasper into an embrace, burying my nose in his thick hair and kissing his temple. Sitting there, listening to the chirrup of the frogs and the occasional muted susurrus of a passing car, I decided that I preferred my frog prince this way. Like turning over a stone to reveal the hidden life scurrying underneath, Jasper had shown me someone even more fascinating than the glamour of his outward persona. Someone I could see just might be willing to settle for a regular bloke like me. I tried to tell him this, but I'm afraid that my words must have come out garbled because he looked up at me with a small smile tugging at his lips.

"So you don't think I'm an utter bastard, then?"

"Of course not! We all do stupid things when we're in love." Just look at me, toiling away in the sodding mud and gathering slimy frogs into buckets, all in the desperate hope that Jasper would smile and offer me a few kind words.

And maybe Jasper could read all of that in my eyes, because he gave me a serious look and leaned in to kiss me softly, the brush of his lips magnified by the glorious tenderness from his earlier kisses.

"Thank you, Simon. For listening and...everything." I was amazed to see his eyes flutter bashfully, before he fixed me with a more heated gaze. "I'm so glad I came back here. To Henley, I mean. I could have chosen anywhere, but I had a few good memories of days out on the river when I was at school. If it hadn't been for that, then I'd probably never have met you."

He was glad he came to Henley because he met me. I took a moment to digest this, a slow smile spreading through my body. I looked out over the dark allotments, the ghostly white of horticultural fleece the only visible landmarks in the gloaming. A cool breeze whispered against my skin and I shivered, hugging Jasper tightly to me.

"I've got some plants at home that need a bit of expert attention. Would you mind coming and having a look at them?" I spoke softly into his ear.

"Umm, yes, of course." He sounded puzzled; possibly a little put out.

"I meant right now. I'm worried that my spider plant isn't

long for this world. If you stay over you could get a look at it first thing in the morning."

Jasper chuckled, his body shaking against me as that smile inside me spread wider and wider, until I was laughing too, giddy with relief and the sense of possibilities spreading open before me, shining golden against the darkness that had bound me for far too long.

"It's pretty hard to kill a spider plant, you know."

"Yes, but I've nearly managed it. I'm in desperate need of your green fingers, and I can probably find a few other uses for them as well." Much more pleasurable ones, I thought, shivering with anticipation.

"Well then, I think it's my positive duty to come and have a look, and see if I can put my fingers to good use in your service." As Jasper's voice purred against my cheek, all I could think of was that tomorrow he'd be waking up next to me, and all was right with the world.

We left the allotments to the frogs, croaking their chorus of sexual frustration into the cool night air.

ADDED
BENEFITS

S. A. Garcia

The portrait of Simon, Brooding Hall's first earl, imitated the Holbein school or, more truthfully, the Holbein nursery school. The amateur brush strokes depicted the earl as cross-eyed, sour, and Quasimodo-ish in appearance. Since portraits flattered a noble, I feared in real life Simon frightened the feathers off a duck.

I herded the tour group to the soaring main hall. A feast of old timbers, lumpy plaster, and assorted artifacts surrounded us in silent historical majesty. The room teased me. I knew this house's history, but I also knew important details escaped me.

"Above the fireplace is a portrait of the first Earl of Alesham. It was..."

I had to interrupt my discourse with some stern politeness. "Billy, please don't touch anything."

The unrepentant brat scowled at me in throat-slitting rancor. "This tour is boring. I want swords and armor, not ugly furniture and stupid old paintings."

"Billy, don't act rude." Billy's mother clamped her hands on his narrow shoulders. Her timid smile was an attempt at mollifying me. "Please do go on, James."

La-da, thanks for the permission to perform my job. Amazing how anger tasted like sour milk. If Billy touched one more antique, I'd tie his wrists together or, better yet, fetch a nasty torture device from the off-limits weapons room. Yes, much more fitting. "The portrait is..."

My words emerged in practiced precision: articulate, educated, and striving for entertainment. Often the entertainment portion failed like stale spotted dick. Unless a tasty family delicacy added spice to a proud Aubusson tapestry, like in 1740 randy Countess Emily merrily shagged the gardener on it, no one cared about the artifact. How sad. At least I cared.

The portrait featuring the murdered-by-his-wife Earl Blake supplied a good yarn. The poor dupe was poisoned by sneaky draughts of mugwort-laced tea. Either his taste buds took a scenic detour or he enjoyed nasty, strong tea.

Reciting my lines, sounding engaging and keeping the scowling Billy in my suspicious sightlines was a juggling problem. As we moved into the hallway, I looked around. "Where's Billy?"

Billy's mum turned toward the sword-encrusted south wall. "He was looking at the swords. My word, where did he go?"

The normally locked door marked "No Admittance" gaped open like the mouth of hell. My heart accelerated in dread but I retained mellow poise. Quite a feat. "Please, people, remain in here and wait for me. No, ma'am, do not come with me." My hand waved Billy's tearful-looking mother away from the door. No need for a parade!

I slipped through the door. Fuck, fuck, fuck! Why did people like children? They always caused mayhem! I slammed a fist into my palm, inhaled a deep breath and stalked my prey. Ancient wormhole-ridden wood paneling and threadbare carpets greeted me. Water stains marred the old plaster.

My fellow guides told me letting tourists stray into the three lower family rooms guaranteed a fast firing, especially since the rooms needed serious renovation. The fine furniture and art sat on display for paying customers. In private the earl and his lone son tolerated faded fabrics and battered furniture more suited to a rummage sale. Nobles often embraced eccentric frugality, so who was I to judge?

If that sneaky brat got me sacked, I would hunt him down. At least the earl was visiting relatives in Scotland. To the caretaker's great distress, three days ago heir Albert arrived from London without warning. So far he remained secreted away in his upper suite. After viewing his portrait on the piano, I desired meeting him, but running into him while he was jogging around the grounds sounded more appealing, especially if he exposed his sweaty, sensational body to the world.

I walked in an open door to the cheerless solarium. Ancient bushy yews towering over the diamond-paned windows conquered the bright afternoon light. I felt sad for the forlorn room.

An unfamiliar voice teased my hearing. My heart tensed. No.

I stepped forward. An awestruck Billy stared at a seated man illuminated by an elderly floor lamp. Lunch remains rested on the battered low table.

Billy and I shared the same instinct. I doubted if he nurtured lust yet but awe, yes indeed, there we shared inspiration. "You see, my fine young buck, this place is dreadfully haunted. The worst ghost loves to terrorize children so if I were you, I'd accompany this handsome gentleman and mind your manners." Amused green eyes tipped up toward me. "There's so much traffic I feel like I dine at Victoria Station."

Albert looked even more heartbreakingly handsome in person. "Forgive me, Lord. Billy, come along immediately." My right fingers tapped Billy's shoulder. I wisely refrained from strangling him.

Despite my resolve to escape, my gaze admired the fleshy presentation draped in stylish black clothing. I swore common Brits were genetically disposed to lusting after nobility; I knew I always imagined holding a pretty noble close in passionate communion. Fair Albert radiated manly pale splendor. As I was dark, during sex we'd create a lovely visual yin/yang.

The blond-haired vision artfully licked his pouty lower lip. "Do you enjoy leading the droll dog-and-pony show around the old pile?" His gaze signaled amorous semaphores.

My word, the tasty young lord flirted with the help? How sensational. Would stuffing Billy into that antique chest define going too far? The brat shouldn't see two men flirting, but what the hell, he'd learn about flirting all too soon. We Brits excelled at sending silent signals. "I quite enjoy the position, Lord Alesham." I licked my own lower lip and let my free hand fall to my left thigh. My fingers twitched to the right.

Albert arched a coy brow. His fingers drifted across his marvelously endowed crotch until they settled on his thighs. His tight, tailored linen trousers advertised potent regal virility. "Splendid. The position owns added benefits for the ambitious gent."

"What a lovely thought, my lord." I cocked my head to the left.

"Indeed." He peered at my brass nameplate. "Ah, James Aston, here's a smashing idea: How about I come out and play lord of the manor for your group?"

Come out? What a tease. I winked. "I feel sure my tour will feel charmed."

Albert rose, stretched his long, lithe torso against his tight black silk shirt and winked back at me. "Grand. I excel at charming audiences both large and small. I prefer more intimate ones but I'll survive. Come along, Billy. Remember, a well-behaved boy might see something special."

The little horror stared in greedy glee. "What?"

A long finger tapped Billy's head. "Tut-tut, if I tell you it won't be so special anymore. Come along and mind your manners. Remember I know exactly where the ghosts hide."

Billy swallowed deeply but refrained from any comment. The lord's child-handling style appealed to me along with his outstanding physical attributes. He guided Billy ahead of him. My caboose position seized the opportunity to squeeze his tempting buttocks.

Albert's left hand swung back and tickled my fingers.

I felt we had made a date. Now my heart accelerated for quite a different reason.

When dashing Lord Albert Alesham entered the main hall, my tour group acted like Prince William had descended from the royal heavens. Drooling *ooohs* and *ahhs* rattled the creaking rafters. "Welcome to my family home. I thought I'd lend James a hand."

Please let that hand land directly on my half-erect cock. I owned no problem allowing Albert to shepherd the group around the entire bottom floor. I supplied facts and he added family fiction. We worked in perfect harmony while flirting up an invisible lust tsunami.

The tour reached a notoriously off-limits area. I arched my brows in query. A commanding finger beckoned to me. "James, let's explore this hallway. Guests, prepare to experience an extra-special ending." Albert pressed a code into the keypad and flung open the old wooden door. "Welcome to Brooding Hall's arms and weapons collection. Inside is a collection rivaling any museum's in rarity. Billy, remember, no touching."

"Absolutely, Lord!"

I felt like I existed in a wonderful hallucination. Albert and I kept a strict watch on everyone's hands. I'd been shown the collection with explicit orders never to speak about it, but arguing with Albert felt unwise. If he wanted to display his inheritance to the tourists, why question him?

The handsome lord answered questions like a born tour guide. After ten minutes I cleared my throat. "I am afraid this concludes our extra-special tour. We're shorthanded this afternoon so I..."

The honey and smoke voice rolled over me. "Fret not, James, I will escort your tour out. Did someone call out sick?"

"The three other guides suffer from stomach flu. I'm the only one on duty today."

"What dreadful luck. Chin up, James. I'll catch up with you during your next tour."

"Thank you, Lord Alesham."

"Certainly, James." His coy wink warmed my cock into a simmer.

The next group patiently waited for me at the front entrance. I made my apologies, collected the fees, and began the tour. Halfway through the tour Albert entered the formal living room. I gestured in dramatic excitement. "Ladies and gentleman, how wonderful, here's Lord Albert Alesham, heir to Brooding Hall."

This enraptured audience clapped in mooning delight. The beaming Albert bowed and spread his arms in regal greeting. "Welcome to Brooding Hall. My friend James is a splendid guide, so if you don't mind, I'll tag along and probably learn something new about my own home."

Now my cock quivered in boiling delight. Once Albert sprinkled his majestic stardust on me, the tour regarded me with wide, receptive eyes. Yes indeed, the day looked better all the time.

Albert moved with the confident grace of someone who accepted the title of walking, talking sex god. He radiated such natural charm I feared the tour group might burn in the light of his sun. Damn, this horny lad wanted to.

Luckily my learned composure cut though my lust and let me perform my duties. Damn, I needed this man. My flits and flirts fell away. I wanted Albert in a profound, passionate manner. Silly but true. Somehow he struck me as a real person needing tender loving care. I sensed his need. I wanted to cure him.

This tour also ended in the extra-special manner. People would tell their friends to visit ancient Brooding Hall since the oh-so-handsome, charming son greeted them and admitted them to secret rooms! I anticipated a demanding summer season. I also anticipated massive disappointment. Today, acting charming suited Albert, but I hardly expected him to make a habit of entertaining the tours. Instead I'd be the one staring down curious tourists while asking, "What ancient weapons collection?"

The last tour of the day awaited me. Albert strolled onto the back terrace, winked at me and pressed his finger to his full lips. I smiled in agreement. A collection of family photos adorned the music room's piano. Inspiration struck me and as I described the photos, I saved my favorite one for last. "This photo is of Earl Alesham's son Lord Albert, who, my word, stands behind you."

The group whirled on collective heel and once again applauded. Two young women eyed him as a potential bed partner. Not today, ladies. This tour guide stood first in line.

Albert needed to market his damned natural allure. That DNA would make him millions. His smile probably tamed rabid lions, deranged dragons, and vicious vipers. It tamed me into perfect lust.

We moved forward. At the pink and white lily arrangement occupying the great hall's corner table, Albert's fingertip tapped a lush, pink bloom. "James, take note. The lilies need to be pinched. Removing the stamens ensures a longer lasting bloom."

I blinked in bewilderment. "I never knew that, Lord."

Albert's vibrant charm plunged into sadness in remarkable speed. "A florist taught me many tricks." Albert reached out and savagely snipped the stamen. The victim fell to the marble tabletop.

The group glanced at each other in confusion.

What the hell just happened? I nattered in cheerful loon style. "How good to learn about lily maintenance. Thank you, Lord. Now through here is the south sitting room. When you enter, note the two splendid sixteenth-century Flemish tapestries on the far wall. They are in immaculate condition."

I glanced back and watched Albert methodically destroy lily stamens. Time to save him. "Lord Alesham, there's an antique clock in here that intrigues me. Can you tell us the history?"

Albert's viridian eyes reflected haunting pain until his smile returned like the sun emerging from a glowering cloud. "Certainly, James." He pressed past me and squeezed my fingers. His whispered "Thank you" rang into my cock. Looked like I was going to end this tour sporting one massive hard-on. Bless my loose-fitting black linen trousers.

I glanced down. Red pollen kissed my fingers. How romantic.

Hot, handsome, and hurting. I knew it. I prayed the royal wonder asked me to stay. Damn, did I pray. I prayed even as my lips recited my historic speech.

To my surprise Albert skipped the extra-special ending. His mood seemed deflated, although he still charmed while departing.

No one felt disappointed since they didn't know they missed anything. I did, though, since my regal beauty didn't issue me a command.

The group crowded into the tiny gift shop, glowing in delight. Too bad we didn't sell photos of the luscious Albert. Perhaps he needed to pose shirtless for a poster. Perhaps I could take the photo.

Count me as smitten. How silly to feel pleased by the brisk sales, but hell, income ensured my job.

I locked the door behind the last smiling tourist and leaned my head against the worn wood. Damn, I never ate lunch. I felt famished, tired and lusty. What a weird combination.

"Dear James, when you finish locking up, care to join me for cocktails in the Secret Garden?"

Balls! I twitched so hard my cock almost suffered dislocation. Albert smiled in radiant apology. "Sorry to startle you, old man. Does a wee drinkie or three appeal to you?"

"Absolutely, Lord...."

A firm right hand halted my servile words. His frown carved lines along his lips. "Albert. Just Albert. Excellent. Come back when you're finished."

I nodded. I didn't trust my voice not to squeak in desire. I closed out the register and locked the proceeds in a safe. I drove to the main gates, punched in the code and their massive weight swung shut.

After work I had planned a run around the lower garden and the pond, a space gloriously sweet smelling from the hay fields surrounding the manor, so jog shorts, a red tank top, and trusty trainers resided in my car. The Earl allowed the guides to treat the grounds as their own, although my three elderly compatriots did nothing more vigorous than sit in the garden and indulge in tea.

Hmm, a healthy run or cocktails with Junior Earl of Fabulous? I practically blinked into my casual clothing. This common brown mouse understood his sexual priorities.

The afternoon sun, so fresh and fine, painted golden brilliance over the surrounding greenery. Light reflected the typical long days of summer glee. Basking in light until 9:30 always thrilled me.

I walked through the main upper garden and waved hello. Bertha, the cook and housekeeper, looked up from examining her kitchen herbs and smiled. "Well, ducks, you're here late."

I struck a saucy pose. "My lady, I respond to a noble cocktail summons."

The housekeeper whistled in racy delight. "Ah then, so you're the reason Albert requested dinner for two on the terrace."

Really? My heart imitated a 747's engine. "That's news to me."

A stern finger scolded me. "Keep mum about it then. Let the laddie surprise you." Bertha shook her head. "It pains me to say he acts right sad of late."

"This afternoon he charmed the socks off three tour groups, although toward the end melancholy tinged his mood."

"I'm not surprised. We wonder why he arrived without notice or why he acts dismal. He's usually such a happy lad. I swear when Albert feels sad it destroys my old heart. This time he won't let his old nanny comfort him so I know it's serious." As she spoke Bertha slid her admiring gaze over my scantily clad body. She owned no qualms over examining my basket. Her smile belonged in the Naughty Hall of Fame. "Hmm, you might be the right perfect boy to perk up Albert's flagging spirits. You're quite the sexy piece. In my opinion I believe you should conduct the tour wearing this hot little outfit. Sales will skyrocket."

"Bertha, darling, you are a dirty old lady."

"And that's the way my Henry likes me. He can never claim boredom, that's for sure!" Bertha performed a lewd bump and grind. Her broad hips almost knocked me into the tall magenta bee balm. Lazy bumblebees fled for safety.

Once I stabilized myself I shook my head. "My dear, you are too much woman for me. Your Henry is a paragon of virility. Now excuse me but I don't want to keep a certain handsome someone waiting."

"Off with you then. Do you like your grilled salmon on the rare side?"

"Yes, that sounds absolutely perfect." I saluted Bertha's smiling face and resumed my stroll. Grilled salmon, eh? My stomach growled in approval.

Pink and white lilies grew to tall, scented decadence. They smelled like gracious sex. The path curved toward the Secret Garden, a compact walled garden displaying pure white blossoms. It was modeled after Vita Sackville-West's famous Sissinghurst white garden. Albert's mother Gwen was a devoted friend of the elderly Vita; some whispered more than mere friend, so she designed this garden as a tribute to Vita's creativity.

If the salacious rumors were true, then sexy Albert took after his mum. Fabulous.

The low arch demanded a duck-down. When I looked up I saw delicious Albert sprawled in a black-cushioned lounge chair. Skimpy red shorts hugged his lean hips. His long blond hair fanned around his head like celestial sun rays. Indeed, I discovered the true sun king hiding in shadowy repose.

"James? Be a sweetie and mix me another lethal G & T."

A glass already sat on the glass patio table perched between the lounge chairs. Might as well reuse it. The battered portable steel bar occupying a wall nook supplied Bombay, Junipero, and

Tanqueray gin along with scotches and vodkas. I could worship at this liquid altar for months and never feel bored. Obviously the earl didn't skimp on his libations. No surprise. "Which brand, handsome lord?"

"Junipero, please. Two lime slices, one ice cube and a kiss of tonic."

Lovely. My budget did not allow for the expensive Junipero so I mixed the same for me. I placed the drinks on the table. Albert reached out and ingested a monumental sip. "You mix a fine cocktail, James. Thanks."

"You offer me a fine presentation, Albert."

"Thank you. I can say the same about you, Studly." He waved his drink at my shorts. "I daresay you are a huge improvement over Bertha. A lovely woman but she insists on baking me scones and fretting over my love life."

I decided sitting so far away from the sun king's warmth didn't suit my intentions. I slid over to his chair and perched thigh to thigh. "Please, Albert, I don't want to fret over it. No, I want to be intimately involved in it."

"Really? Why?"

"Why not?"

His emerald stare competed with the vibrant ivy's hue. "How do you know I'm not already involved?"

"With your florist?"

Albert's fair skin flushed in epic embarrassment. "Ah, apologies for my rather erratic performance. Quite an open wound, you see. Armando the amorous florist abandoned me for a wealthy young sheik. Three years together, then boom, Mr. Baby Oil Wells stole him. I felt like a crash victim so I fled home." The rich blue skies soaring above us intensified his gaze.

How could anyone reject this legendary man? I leaned forward and gently kissed frowning lips. "Considering you are one of the finest men in existence, I don't understand how anyone could leave you."

Albert returned my kiss. His fingers trailed into my long black curls. Mmm. I snuggled down beside him. Our kiss throttled into sexy high gear. Tongues said hello. Logical mind asked, *Did this chair feel sturdy enough to accept a flash fuck?*

We raced along in merry glory. Our close contact created fragrant sex sweat, ahh, sweet ambrosia. Capable muscles flexed against my fingertips. I pressed nearer.

Suddenly Albert drew away from me and sighed in distress. "Sorry, James, I need to vent to someone who understands. Know why Armando dumped me? I sport a jolly noble title but the estate is poor. In fact the estate approaches bankruptcy. That explains the tours. If we show off the grand old place, we receive funding, plus tours bring in enough cash for basic maintenance. My damned selfish grandfather was a serial gambler so my poor father inherited a mountain of debt. We've sold off all the acreage excluding the final seven. In 1970 we owned five hundred acres. Now it's down to seven." He gulped back too much of his drink.

Ridiculous. My fingers trailed against his firm belly. "I don't care what you own, I care about you. Listen, I attend Oxford on a history scholarship. My marks scored me this job. This year I graduate with a master's in medieval history, the first in my family to ever achieve such a honor. I hardly lust after wealth but I do lust after you. I have ever since I saw your photo on the piano. You need me to cure you." Time for my audacious suggestion, although I knew it smashed a boulder into the sexy proceedings. "Your weapons collection is astonishing. Has it been authenticated?"

Albert blinked in surprise. "Authenticated? Yes, my grandfather already looted it. It's full of reproductions, just like the manor's painting and tapestry collection. He sold plenty to private collectors for a quick pound."

Ah, that solved the grand hall's mystery. "Are you sure? I know what I saw. During the second tour I really examined the items. They don't look like reproductions."

His strong fingers gripped my arm in excitement. "Let's take a closer look."

Of course I wanted to explore Albert's tasty torso but I also wanted to help his pride. After mutual sips, we abandoned our drinks and marched to the weapons room. "May I touch?"

"Of course."

"Look, this crossbow is from the twelfth century. It's in immaculate condition. Priceless. I can't believe it's fake. That battered sword might even be from the Bronze Age. Amazing. You need someone more adept than me to judge the value, but a museum would offer an impressive sum." I turned and caressed Albert's wavy mane. "You hide a historical treasure chest down here. Use it."

"Use me first." Albert pulled me close. Our lips spoke volumes. Fingers located pressure points in teasing passion. The cold stone floor pressed against my lust-flushed skin. Lips wrestled in glory. Albert's fingers reached in and grasped my weeping cock. "May I own the pleasure of exploring you?"

"Absolutely." I sprawled on the hard floor and shimmied off my shorts. My cock waved in invitation. I held up a small tube of Vaseline toward my junior earl.

"What a prepared boy. Do you always travel ready to be adored?"

"No, my right heel has a rough spot so I apply this before I run."

Albert looked puzzled. "I circuit the pond a few times a week. Today I decided to skip the effort for more delicious pursuits."

"Wise boy." His fingers felt cool and fine stroking my heated cock. They looked like vanilla branches teasing milk chocolate. "Daddy would kill me if he knew how we plan on baptizing the weapons room."

"I think he'd fire my ass in record time."

"No, I'm about to fire your succulent ass, Sweetie." He slid his palms under my cheeks and dug in his nails. After a frenzied kiss he slid on his condom. "I confess I came prepared for action. You watched me in a luscious manner too hard to resist." His lips attacked mine again. He draped his body atop of me in rib-to-rib crush. Our cocks mashed between us. "Are you comfortable?"

"I love being your mattress, Albie."

"Albie. How sweet, Jimmy. I love it." Albert drew back and danced his cock to my lips. "You own such soft, divine lips."

I nuzzled the hard shaft pressed against my cheek and applied my tongue in stern lashings. I never enjoyed attacking Latex but Albie's thin condom tasted like mint. What a considerate lord. When I rolled his thick cock between my chin and chest, Albie purred in delight. He shimmied back down my torso. His cock slapped down to thrust against mine. His palms ground into my chest muscles.

I maneuvered my ass against his cock until Albie hefted my shins to his shoulders. Light pinches punctuated his hoarse laughter. His fingers tickled my lips. "Naughty James, are you asking me something?"

"Will the lord of the manor show me his sword play?"

"Ooh, cliché! Adorable." Vaseline swirled between our cocks. Albie skimmed two exploratory fingers deep inside. My resulting muscle clench told him now.

Without further commotion Albie entered me. My head hit the stone floor. During a stellar fuck the waking world always turned blurry. Nothing felt normal. Quite invigorating. This afternoon

Junior Earl Fabulous fucked me into wild interplanetary confusion. Comets blasted past my eyes. Stars died and blossomed into new life. Before lust devoured my remaining coherency I blessed the silly florist for tossing this vigorous bloomer to the rubbish heap. Albie's talented cock sprouted extra appendages to ensure all the proper inner contact. No doubt in my mind; Albie took after his mother.

All too fast I came in screaming delight. Albie took his time, he swirling his cock inside me until he collapsed in defeat.

My fingers tangled in his blond lengths. My audacity discovered new heights. "This wild family needs a proper written history. I can begin tomorrow."

Albie nipped my nose. "You are the perfect man for the job."

I clenched my inner muscles. "I am the perfect man for many jobs here."

"Aren't you the bold one! You'll be pleased to hear tonight you're the perfect man to dine with me."

"I accept the offer."

Naughty lips teasing my nipple forced a gasp from my arched neck. "This weekend you are the perfect man to accompany me to my cousin's wedding."

Damn! "I'm scheduled to ..."

A hand dismissed any problems. "Not any more. You deserve time off for stellar behavior. The tedious event is at Everhampton Castle, and let me say the place brims with sexy tryst possibilities." Albie's teeth nibbled my lower lip. "Say yes. Keep me from falling into another depression. Keep me happy." His lips attacked mine. "Stay with me, James. Heal me. Be mine."

This common brown mouse never refused a royal command from his perfect sun king.

Never ever.

SECRET SERVICE

Gregory L. Norris

His name was Duke—Brandon Joseph Duke—but the senator knew he was a prince from the moment they met.

The senator felt the first bullet streak past his face, close enough to displace air and heat the skin of his cheek, a fraction of a second before the gun's report stung at his ear. An instant later, Duke was on top of him, covering the senator's shorter, older body with his mass of muscles. Through the cacophony of a hundred things happening all at once, the screams, the clatter of chairs and footsteps, and the second thunderclap, proof of another gunshot, the senator heard Duke barking out orders.

"Exit points, *now*," he said, his voice a commanding baritone. "Take him down, any way you have to!"

Then Duke was leaning over the senator's face, and the agent's cheek, showing a hint of five o'clock shadow half an hour early, at four-thirty on a sunny summer afternoon, brushed against him, unleashing a flock of butterflies in the senator's stomach. Enhancing the sensation further was Duke's scent, which filled the senator's next desperate breath. It was a real man's smell; the senator detected a trace of soap and sweat and the clean natural cologne of masculine skin, which he recognized as the result of adrenaline mixing with testosterone, pulsing through his protector's bloodstream, emanating up through the epidermis. Intoxicating. The smell of Brandon Duke.

For a few brief and blinding seconds, the senator only thought of the Secret Service agent who'd tackled him down onto the grass, not the reason why. Duke's cheek rested against the senator's face. Both of Duke's arms embraced him, along with one leg. That leg…the senator was a leg man. And a foot man. And an ass man. And a loose, low-hanging nut man, of course…and he figured his prince's were about the biggest, lowest-hanging pair in the history of valorous knights. But a man's legs and feet pushed even more powerful buttons in his DNA than genitalia alone, the love of both hardwired into his sexual identity.

Duke's legs, beneath those crisp black dress slacks, would be magnificent. Muscular without being showy, the legs of a man who played baseball and hockey, hairy in the proper thickness, the kind that looked great when he jogged beside the president or took to the shooting range in a pair of camouflage cutoffs. And those feet—Duke's black wingtips on the same leg thrown protectively over the senator's ass was a big one, a twelve or thirteen in size. Sometimes, at least in the senator's rapid fantasy, Duke went jogging without sweat socks and his feet smelled hot and wonderful after he peeled off his sneakers, the buttery sweat rising off his toes the sexiest of smells on a man's body. He imagined Duke dressed only in blue jeans, barefoot, unshaved, walking around his apartment en route to jerking off into a discarded sock.

Duke shifted and the senator swore he could feel the other man's meaty thickness humping against his spine and, to his shock, his own cock began to stiffen, pinned atop the grass.

The fantasy ended too soon. Duke stood, taking the senator with him. From the corner of his eye, the senator saw Duke make one of those military hand signals, a pumped fist followed by two flying fingers. Those fingers...they were long, strong, the nails neatly trimmed, the backs just hairy enough. The senator knew the man's feet would be no less perfect, sexy in a way that part of a man's anatomy wasn't supposed to be according to society's standards, but was by his own personal beliefs.

Duke started running, holding onto the senator's arm with one hand, the other drawing his service revolver from its shoulder holster. They sprinted away from the overturned podium where the senator's town meeting-style open forum on repealing "Don't Ask, Don't Tell" had barely gotten started before coming to a chaotic end, over to a black sedan, where two other security men waited. The tinted windows were likely bulletproof. Not lost on the senator was the way Duke loomed behind him, putting his body in the way of harm. A modern knight. A prince. On the mad dash to safety, the senator's heart surrendered. He instantly loved this man, this hero.

Duke tossed him through the open door and into the back seat. As he landed, the senator looked up and stole a clear look at Brandon Duke's face, recording it forever. Face to face, he was even more handsome than cheek to cheek; perhaps the handsomest man the senator had ever seen. He certainly was at that moment, with the dark cowlicks and spikes of his intentional bed-head, his square jaw and classic good looks, the trace of prickly shadow and his eyes, eyes so richly green they reminded the senator of emeralds. The man's charcoal jacket and crisp white button-down, black tie, and slacks had, he figured, started the afternoon straight and spotless. Now, they bore wrinkles and grass stains, but the effect was curiously even more attractive, that edge of dishevelment enhancing the whole like the grit that results in creating pearls.

Their eyes met. To the senator's surprise, they also held. In that bottled gaze, the air grew heavier and harder to breathe. The wind carried Duke's heady male scent into the sedan, dispelling the new car smell. From the corner of his eye, the senator noticed Duke's hairy throat as it knotted under the influence of a swallow, as if the protector were feeling the same connection and attraction as the protected. The senator knew that this would be their final private moment together for some time before the media and media relations took over, putting every blink and word beneath the microscope.

Then the senator caught an expanding bloom of red color from the periphery.

"You're hit," one of the other Secret Service men said.

Duke slammed the sedan's door, and the senator's heart jumped into his throat. The thunderclap, in some ways, was louder than the report that had led him to this moment. Duke turned and was gone. The senator realized that Brandon Joseph Duke had taken the bullet meant for him.

Brett McConnell, the senator's press secretary, moved over to him and leaned in. "I have to go out there again and address the networks, but this is the latest. The gunman's name is L'Ecuyer. Tillman L'Ecuyer. Real piece of work."

"I guessed that much."

The senator glanced at the TV screen. As if on cue, the same twenty seconds of footage he'd already seen played out again, that of the police dragging the gunman away while he shouted that the Almighty despised men of the same-sex persuasion, only not in such eloquent terms.

"We're coming to you live from Prosperity Park, where a

gunman has tried to assassinate the controversial, openly gay
senator responsible for leading the attempt to repeal the 'Don't
Ask, Don't Tell' military protocol law...."

The senator recognized the talking head from the nightly
national news, which had cut in early. The park, a public green
space dedicated to the ideals of equal rights, was quickly being
transformed into a traffic jam of satellite trucks and camera
crews. Ironic, considering the senator was no longer there but at
the makeshift command center where his staffers were gathered
to deal with the crisis and resulting media blitz.

"We're also receiving reports that one of the Secret Service
guards assigned to protect the senator may have been shot by
L'Ecuyer. We're expecting an official statement from the senator
shortly...."

A shiver tumbled down the senator's spine. "What about the
prince?"

"The prince?" McConnell parroted.

The senator blinked. "I meant Duke. Brandon Duke, the
agent who risked his life out there."

"We've got a call into the hospital for an update on his condition."

"You can put in another one, and then get my car ready. Just
as soon as we're done here, I want you to take me there."

"To the hospital?"

"Yes."

"But—"

"Come on," the senator said, reaching for his jacket.

His own words and voice from the TV greeted the senator as he
approached the door to Duke's hospital room.

"The incredible valor shown by this man, this hero, will not
go unrewarded. I consider his example proof that, despite the

challenges we Americans face in today's dangerous times, we are moving forward to a safer, more civilized future, and that vanguards like Brandon Duke will march with us to rise to the occasion when called upon."

Navigating through the media, which had begun camping outside the hospital, had been difficult enough. Getting approval to pass the hospital staff was even harder, but McConnell succeeded. Now, the last barrier between the senator and his protector was a pair of rugged suits, similar in build, but nowhere nearly as handsome. One guarded the door. The other sat in that classic stance of cowboys and tough guys, straddling the chair backward. Fellow Secret Service agents, the senator assumed. He greeted the gatekeeper. Duke and the other men, engaged in a spirited discussion about how Duke would become the new Hollywood poster boy, the sexiest man alive, and the star of his own reality TV show, looked up.

The senator's heart galloped. "Hi," he said.

The smile on Duke's face widened slightly. "Senator," he said.

In quick order, the senator absorbed the details of his surroundings: your basic hospital room, two windows with the drapes down, a mechanical bed. What wasn't typical was the room's lone patient. Duke sat with the back of the bed raised, his legs crossed beneath a top sheet. His clothes hung on a peg, his shoes and black socks were in an electric blue patient's belongings bag beneath them.

The ridiculous hospital gown did little to mar the senator's earlier impression of the man. He tried not to stare at the lush thatch of dark chest hair poking over the johnny's neck, or the equally magnificent tuft of fur visible beneath Duke's uninjured arm. The same arm bore a Celtic cross, in turquoise ink. The other was wrapped in a clean white bandage, over the upper puff of muscles. An intravenous snaked down to and around his wrist.

"Antibiotics," Duke said, as if reading his thoughts. More likely, the handsome hero was tracking the senator's gaze, part of his training for the job. "The bullet only grazed my arm, but they have to make sure there's no infection."

"Good deal," the senator said.

"Come on in, Sir," Duke said. Then he addressed his buddies. "You don't mind giving us a few, do you?"

The men excused themselves, saying it was time they hustled anyway. Both shook the senator's hand on the way out.

"Brett, do you mind waiting outside?"

The senator's press secretary said he didn't and closed the door behind him. That left the two men alone again in a tenebrous silence. The senator's bedroom browns fell into the hypnotic pull of Duke's emerald greens.

Duke aimed his good thumb at the vacated chair. "Have a seat, please."

The senator shuffled over. "Thanks."

Duke smiled, nodded. This close to him, the scent of the Duke's skin was obvious and magical, the proof of Duke's excitement coming clearer to the senator than when they'd been locked together on the ground, one's body atop the other's. It rose clearly in the senator's breaths, seeming to grow stronger by the second. Was such a thing possible? Duke was a Secret Service agent, likely ex-military, a jock. Or had the day's events scrambled the senator's mind into mixing up the signals?

"And thanks for what you did."

"It was my pleasure, Sir."

The senator said, "You don't have to be so formal."

Duke shrugged. "Maybe I like the sound of it."

Was that another misread signal? The word *Sir* carried a lot of weight in public, but even more so in private.

"You saved my life," he settled for instead.

"Just doing my job."

The senator's eyes broke free and wandered down to the thick patch of chest hair before going back up, recording the details of Duke's lips, an impressive set, the lower slightly plumper than its topside twin. What he wouldn't give to kiss and be kissed by them.

"And I'd do it again," Duke continued. "I admire you, Sir."

The senator drew in a deep breath and his lungs filled with Duke's arousing scent. "You do?"

Duke nodded. "I admire what you stand for. That you know who you are, you're proud of it, no apologies. That takes real balls. I wish I had your sac."

Suddenly, the senator understood completely. Ex-military. Don't Ask, Don't Tell. He wasn't hallucinating the agent's scent of arousal or misreading signals. An ugly incident had brought them together, but what had resulted could lead to something closer, something beautiful.

"You've got a great set already, I imagine," the senator said. "You're a prince, Duke. If there's anything I can ever do..."

And then, Duke leaned over and kissed him, full on the lips.

The taste of the other man's mouth was beyond addictive. The senator's shock passed and he kissed back, wondering how he'd ever lived without Brandon Duke in his life. How would he be able to live without him if this moment turned out to be nothing more than a fantasy suffered during a gunshot wound or as part of a concussion sustained after being body-slammed to the ground?

He laid a hand on Duke's chest and searched for his heart-beat. The senator's fingers wandered to the place where the hospital gown ended and hairs sprouted. The coarse sensation beneath his fingertips was real. So was what happened next, when Duke's good hand covered his and guided it downward, over his stomach and the firm muscles of his six-pack, toward a destination even harder.

The senator's fingers gripped Duke's erection and gave it a flute. Duke moaned around their next kiss. The senator tugged at the hem of the johnny, raising it up and exposing the fur-ringed O of his protector's belly button, and so much more.

Hair, thick and musty, wreathed a meaty cock, a real man's, with a shaft thickest at the middle covered in dings and thin blue veins. Duke's piece bore a classic fireman's helmet for a head. A set of hairy nuts that exceeded the senator's earlier expectation hung loosely beneath.

Breaking the kiss took the greatest effort. On his way down, the senator noticed the length of leg his fumbling had exposed. Hairy, like he'd hoped, an athlete's leg, a prince's. What he would do to Duke's legs with his fingers and tongue. And the man's feet, as well—he planned to sniff and suck each toe, as though they were smaller versions of his protector's dick. But first...

He opened wide enough and accepted the head of Duke's cock between his lips. A real man's taste ignited on the senator's tongue, and the musky sweat of ripe balls filled his next sip of breath. He couldn't believe what was happening on this day, when a madman had tried to steal his life; the day in which he'd barely cheated death thanks to the chivalry of a handsome prince. Now, here he was, sucking the cock of his ideal man, the handsomest man alive.

The senator spit out Duke's thickness and drew in a ball, gently swirling his tongue around it before showing the same attention to its mate. Duke moaned and stretched out, flexing his toes beneath the sheet. One foot slipped free and into view.

Brandon Duke's feet were the sexiest the senator had ever seen. Oh yes, this had turned out being a day for the history books.

Duke groaned. The senator licked both hairy low hangers on the return of his lips to Duke's cock. He couldn't tell how long Brett would be able to guard the door before the hospital staff barged through. And the media.... There was a crisis brewing out there, a real shit storm. He and his prince were living on short time.

He sucked, and Duke's cock rewarded him with the salty-sour first few drops of pre-cum. The senator toyed with his protector's balls, and the juice flowed thicker.

"Yeah," Duke sighed. "Keep going, Sir. Just like that. I'm close."

The senator sucked. Breathless, minutes later, Duke placed his good hand on the back of the senator's head, thrust in, and unloaded. The senator swallowed, but not all of it. Rising, he planted a kiss on Duke's lips, thinking it the proper thing to do. Duke kissed back, unfazed by the act of tasting his own seed. Their lips locked together, and Duke cupped the senator's face, a tender but also possessive gesture.

"Thank you, Sir," Duke said once they parted.

The senator smiled and caressed Duke's spent yet still thick member, aware of how hard his dick hung in the prison of his pants. "It was the least I could do to thank the hero who saved my life."

"Which was the least I could do for the hero who saved mine," said the prince.

The senator nodded. He understood. He also sensed the beginning of something good here with his princely protector, his handsome Duke.

PRINCE OF DARKNESS

Jay Starre

Dario Clemente Di Niccoli stood and bowed as the young prince entered his office. From behind his oak desk, he extended a hand to the man and offered a semi-sincere smile. He had heard tales of this Genoan aristocrat, a refugee from the turmoil in northern Italy. They called him the prince of darkness.

"Signor Di Niccoli, you have been recommended by a mutual acquaintance. One whom I will not name, as I am sure you will understand."

The voice was pleasant and the smile engaging. Lustrous black hair fell to his shoulders while a trimmed beard of equal darkness framed a round face. Direct dark eyes under ink-black brows hovered above a bold nose. Tall and broad shouldered, he stood confidently on muscular thighs outlined dramatically in navy blue stockings. He held a dark green coat of fine lamb's wool in one arm.

"I understand perfectly, Prince Da Conti. And what is the sum you require today?"

Dario dealt with people of all stations and walks of life, but especially with the aristocracy in their need for loans or other services his bank offered. Discretion and generous repayment schedules were usually what these princes were after.

The dark eyes sparkled and the smile grew into a brilliant beam between the full lips. "Ah, a man of directness. I find that quality lacking in so many."

He went on to name a substantial, but not outrageous, sum. Dario quickly calculated the risk and after a brief hesitation agreed. It took only a few minutes to write out the accord and offer it to the seated prince for his signature.

"Of course I will repay you sooner if things go my family's way in the summer offensives. I have recently received optimistic reports from Genoa."

That is what they all said, Dario reflected. And sometimes it was true—as often as there were losers in war and politics, there were winners.

As the prince rose with paper in hand, he spontaneously reached out and grasped Dario's hand. "My sincerest gratitude, Signor Di Niccoli."

To the young banker's total surprise, the prince bent over his desk and kissed his hand. His eyes remained locked on Dario's as his red lips continued to smile generously.

Then he whirled away and practically flew out of the room. Athletic thighs carried him buoyantly, almost flamboyantly. He most likely deserved his reputation as a rake, but he was definitely a charmer.

Smiling, Dario first rubbed his tingling hand where those full lips had touched, then slipped a hand down to squeeze the stiff bulge in his crotch where the prince's charm had proved most effective.

After that initial meeting Dario did not see the handsome

prince again for a month. It was early May, and the flowers of spring were blooming in every pot on every balcony as he strode down the narrow alleys of Naples toward his destination that late afternoon.

The tavern where he was to meet his associate was infamous for its debauched patrons. These young aristocrats more often than not ended up being carted home bruised or wounded after drunken brawls.

It was also a place where clients could be found. Not that he and his fellow banker would solicit openly. Merely being seen, and gossiped about, would serve well enough to garner business in the following days.

The establishment was rowdy already. He found his friend at a table strategically chosen on the lower floor. They could be seen but were not in the direct line of fire from the carousing patrons on the upper floor.

Effort had been made to create a decor of sorts. The walls were stuccoed in a pleasant ochre while alcoves boasted statuary in the earlier Roman style, fakes of course. The tables were sturdy oak affairs while the floor was layered with fresh straw to soak up the spilled food, wine, puke, and blood.

A marble bar where busy maids and a burly bartender prepared drinks separated the two levels. The kitchen's open doorway allowed the smell of roasting meat to entice the patrons.

Although he ate heartily, Dario drank only watered wine, and that sparingly. Not that he was against drink or drunkenness per se, he was merely cheap. Food was a necessity, wine was not.

He did not notice the Da Conti prince at first. It was his voice that eventually caught the banker's attention. He was singing, loudly yet admirably in tune. He appeared above the crowd a moment later as he climbed atop the table he shared with other rowdy friends who joined him in bawdy song.

Dario watched along with the crowd as the prince cavorted for his audience, performing a jig as his compatriots cheered him on. He wore a brocaded emerald tunic that emphasized his broad shoulders and fit snugly around his narrow waist. Crimson stockings clung to his fine thighs and muscular calves.

His face was flushed, deepening the sultry bronze of his skin. With that black hair and beard it was easy to see how he had come to be named the prince of darkness.

Dario himself was fair-haired and green-eyed thanks to the Gauls in his ancestry. Like many, he was attracted to his opposite. The Da Conti prince seemed his opposite in every way.

He would never have dared to dance and sing in front of a leering crowd. He was embarrassed merely to watch. Still, he admired the comely prince who was at ease with all eyes on him. When Da Conti finished his song with a call for a round of drinks for his friends, again Dario found himself both appalled and envious.

Generous and carefree with his money—or at least generous with Dario's employer's money. He squirmed in his seat as he contemplated that careless squandering of coin. It was so much against his own frugal nature.

"Do you know why they call him the prince of darkness?"

His friend interrupted his thoughts with a tap on the arm. Dario flushed as he realized how he had been gawking at the cavorting prince. "Because of his dark hair and dusky skin?"

Even as he said it, he braced for unpleasant truths. Emile was a keen gossip. The brown-haired banker licked his lips as he prepared to reveal his secrets.

"Prince Adolfo Cesarino Da Conti has engaged in at least a dozen duels—killing a man in one! And this just during his past six months in Naples. Who knows what deviltry he engaged in back in Genoa? It is said he was banished by his family for his outrageous behavior."

This sounded bad, but unfortunately during these times not so unusual. Dueling was as common as war, a way of life for the aristocracy. Still, Emile was not finished with his tale, and Dario prepared himself for worse.

"It is said," and the young banker hesitated as he again licked his lips and leaned in to whisper this last, "the Da Conti prince engages in depraved sexual liaisons! Rough sex of the most brutish kind. He is a savage in the bedroom. And, believe it or not, he has left a trail of broken hearts in his callous wake!"

The stiffening in his crotch became a full-out throbbing erection. Dario's blush turned crimson, and not just due to those lewd revelations, but also because of the way it made him feel.

A disturbance from the upper floor caught their attention. It was the prince again, only this time he was not singing but fending off a drunkard spewing angry accusations.

"The bastard son of Cardinal Rosario," Emile whispered. "One of Da Conti's jilted lovers! This will be delicious."

It appeared as if a duel was imminent as the burly bastard berated the prince with rising rudeness, then raised an arm and slapped him soundly across the cheek. The raucous crowd fell suddenly silent.

Dario found himself holding his breath, his prick stiffer than ever. But Da Conti's reaction was far from what he and the crowd anticipated. He literally turned the other cheek before reaching out and embracing his fuming opponent. Laughing, he pulled the man down beside him and began to chatter gaily with him and his friends.

Disappointed, the crowd resumed its carousing. Dario and Emile continued their meal and drinks for another hour before they rose to take their leave. Just then, a figure appeared out of the milling throng to accost them.

"Signor Di Niccoli! I am so pleased to see you! Earlier I spotted that crown of glorious blond from across the room but have been too occupied with the attentions of friends and jealous lovers to greet you. But now that you are about to leave, I must at least bid you good night!"

With that, Prince Da Conti swept the stunned banker into his arms and kissed him quite soundly on the cheek, then to Dario's complete astonishment, on the lips as well.

Dario realized the aristocrat was drunk, yet still his prick shot up stiffly as the prince pressed his muscular body against his own. He mumbled something polite as he gazed into those dark orbs with mesmerized shock.

Da Conti released him, bowed, and melted back into the crowd.

Emile went on and on about it as they traipsed their way home through the meandering alleys of the city, but Dario barely heard a word. His thoughts were in a turmoil.

He was both attracted and repelled by Da Conti's dark qualities. In any other man, prince or not, repulsion would have won out. But Adolfo had kissed his hand, gazed into his eyes, complimented him, charmed him—and finally this night embraced and kissed him—in public!

He was more handsome than a Botticelli angel and so full of life it seemed to burst out of him. With those poetic thoughts in mind, Dario finally managed to laugh at himself. The prince was merely drunk, and not above kissing young blond men who caught his eye.

Nevertheless, when he crawled into his bed that night he could not help but stroke his aching manhood into an ecstatic release. A sin, but a lesser one compared to the lewd thoughts he entertained regarding the prince of darkness and himself, kissing again, and perhaps even naked.

The very next day he received an engraved invitation to supper at Prince Da Conti's villa.

He suspected that the aristocrat required another loan, thus the ebullient greeting and kiss the previous evening. It would not be the first time a wealthy client invited him to dinner or into his bed. Dario was comely, with soft features and a quiet demeanor that soothed his customers and belied his ambitious nature. His smooth cheeks, dimpled chin, and button nose also contributed to the notion that he was very young and very naive. He was not. At twenty-five, he was well educated and vastly experienced in his chosen profession.

To save money, he rode out of the city along the curve of the Bay of Naples on his horse rather than renting a carriage. The late afternoon sun sparkled on the sea and cast emerald auras around the conical cypress trees that stood along either side of the road.

Verdant spring growth climbed the slopes of Mount Vesuvius, creating a glorious backdrop for the whitewashed Da Conti villa. He reined in his horse before a profusion of lilacs that assaulted his nostrils with their fragrance. A lad appeared to direct him through the gate and then disappeared toward the stable with his mount.

Not a palace, but a well-kept home nonetheless boasting a plethora of expensive furnishings and fine gardens. It was not rented but belonged to the prince's Genoan family. It was Dario's job to know these things.

He found Prince Da Conti in the kitchen. Merrily chopping spring vegetables with a chubby cook at his side, he greeted Dario brandishing a sharp knife and a gorgeous smile.

"Signor Di Niccoli! Welcome to my family's humble abode. As you can see, we are preparing supper. Would you like to help? Antonio, fetch my handsome friend an apron."

The prince was delighted to see that Dario was well acquainted with kitchen tasks. "I cook for myself," Dario explained, then found himself admitting more than he intended. "It saves me a lot of money not to pay a cook."

The prince laughed heartily while clapping his own cook on the back. "I should do the same! What do you think, Antonio?"

The fat cook rolled his eyes and deigned not to reply.

The meal was prepared and to Dario's continued astonishment he and the prince set the table and served it up themselves without the aid of a bevy of servants. Never had Dario seen any aristocrat cook or set a table himself.

"I would prefer you call me Adolfo. May I call you Dario? Do you like the olives? These sweet ones have been marinated in honey and peach vinegar. These tart ones have been soaked in local herbs and a sour cherry wine. I admit I am a connoisseur of olives. I spent my childhood at our family's olive orchards following around the laborers and making a pest of myself. If I was brave enough, I would escape Italy and spend the rest of my life growing olives. And perhaps grapes too! Do you not like the wine?"

Dario was amused and bemused. Their conversation was easy and pleasant. Although he was naturally shy, his profession required him to feign a more outgoing personality. Usually listening with an interested ear sufficed. In the charming company of this dark prince, he found himself saying more than ever before. "The wine is excellent, Adolfo. But I would rather not overindulge as I am enjoying our evening so much I prefer not to vomit or pass out."

The prince's laughter and sparkling gaze encouraged Dario to admit even more. "If I was brave I would escape my chains as well. I would join you in that olive orchard and spend the remainder of my days with paint brush in hand."

Once it was out, he could not take it back. And strangely, he did not wish to. It suddenly did not matter if he joined the ranks of so many others who had fallen under the dark prince's alluring spell. He was being honest for the first time in his life.

With a smile on his lips and a glint in his eyes that could not be mistaken, Adolfo rose and stepped around the edge of the table to lean down and plant his mouth squarely over Dario's.

Arms pulled him to his feet and enveloped him in a crushing embrace. Emile's whispered gossip came back to him now as he conjured up images of savage and wild lovemaking.

Instead, he experienced the kiss of his life.

Adolfo's tongue slid between Dario's gasping lips. Long and pointed, it darted around eagerly as plump lips pressed against his own to open his mouth wider. He snorted in the same air that Adolfo exhaled, their nostrils flaring in a matching rhythm.

The prince sucked in Dario's tongue, chewing lightly on it. He moaned loudly as he began to undress his guest right there in the dining hall amid the flickering candles with the evening breeze wafting in from the open balcony.

Never breaking that wet kiss, Adolfo unbuttoned and unlaced the front of Dario's woolen tunic, then tore it back off his arms. Dario submitted with groans, trembling from head to toe as his torso was bared and that sucking mouth continued to control his own.

Once he had Dario naked from the waist up, Adolfo seemed to grow less rushed as he began to stroke the banker's pale shoulders and arms. Unrelenting in his domination of the blond's mouth, his fingers trailed over the muscles of his upper back and sturdy neck, then slipped between them over Dario's smooth torso. The fingers were long and elegant, but the palms were callused due to his athletic lifestyle. The softness of those fingertips, and the roughness of those palms titillated the groaning banker in a way he had not previously experienced.

His nipples began to throb and swell, much as his prick had already. Quivering like a strung bow, he emitted a wild moan as those rough palms began to rub lightly against the swollen nubs. Dario arched his back and pushed into those palms as he opened his mouth wide and took in Adolfo's tongue as deep as possible.

The prince pulled back slightly, now teasing Dario's gaping pink lips with the tip of his tongue. At the same time he began to tweak Dario's nipples with his fingertips. The sensation was unbelievable.

Those fingertips alternated between tugging lightly, rubbing the pointed tips, then squeezing gently, all while Adolfo's tongue stroked his open mouth and wet lips.

Dario's own hands had gripped the prince's slim waist almost helplessly as he surrendered to that all-consuming kiss and nipple fondling. Now they came alive with a need of their own. He dared to unbutton the prince's tunic with trembling fingers and then dive between the open silk to press his palms against the hot amber flesh beneath.

So firm! The prince's stomach was rippled with muscle, and his chest was round and solid. The flesh was lightly furred and hot to the touch. Dario settled both hands over the mounds of the powerful chest and felt the prince's heart beating beneath his palms.

His own chest tingled and throbbed. His nipples were growing steadily hotter as those fingertips tweaked and rubbed them. His thighs trembled. He wondered how long it could go on, wishing it might be forever, when the hands on his chest moved.

One came up and clasped the back of his neck under the thick curls of his hair. The other dropped down to his waist and tore at the strings of his stockings. The hand behind his neck pressed his face firmly against Adolfo's as the prince once more enveloped his mouth with a wet kiss. Tongue stabbed deep into his mouth as fingers seized the waistband of his stockings and shoved downward.

He was being stripped! Held in place by that hand on the back of his neck, and wet mouth covering his own, he groaned and shuddered as his bare prick reared outward. His stockings were pushed to his knees and the hand moved suddenly behind him to seize a cheek of his full buttocks.

One hand gripped his neck while the other gripped his ass-cheek. Still that slobbering kiss went on.

His nipples still burned from the prince's manipulation, but now his ass was the focus of Adolfo's attentions. The hand on his smooth ass-cheek slid over the full mound and toward the deep crack. Dario moaned around the tongue in his mouth as fingers stroked the clenched crack then began to delve into it.

Even with his stockings tangled around his knees, he managed to spread his feet wider. The hand slid into the parted valley. Fingers found and stroked the entrance to his gut. Dario felt suddenly lightheaded as he snorted for air and began to squat over those fingers.

There was no denying his need. There was no shame, no regret. He willed his ass-lips to part and allowed a finger to slide into him. Not forcefully, but steadily, that finger wormed up into him, deeper and deeper. Once buried in his gut, it began to massage, twisting and frigging slowly and purposefully.

That kiss sucked all resistance out of him. His sphincter transformed into a pulsing cavern that welcomed a second, then a third finger. He had never felt so stuffed!

Quaking between those two hands and the devouring mouth, he allowed his hands to slide down Adolfo's muscular torso and drop to his crotch. There he discovered the lengthy steel of the prince's fuck-sword.

It was stiff and twitching. Beneath the wool of his stockings, it pushed outward with jerking need. With those fingers rummaging deep in his bowels, and his own hands massaging the substantial girth of Adolfo's prick, it was time for Dario to make his plea.

He broke their kiss with a slobbering smack. "Fuck me, Adolfo! I need your prick inside me!"

The Da Conti prince laughed aloud. "Gladly. Let us retire to my bed chambers."

He stepped back, hands abandoning neck and ass. Dario shuddered as those fingers slipped from his asshole, leaving behind an aching pit of need. He had never before wanted, needed, to get fucked so badly.

Adolfo smiled into Dario's eyes as he removed his tunic and blouse, boots and stockings right there in the dining room, tossing them aside to join Dario's discarded tunic. The banker followed his lead, surprisingly unashamed to be revealing his nude body before the roaming eyes of his dark prince.

Adolfo reached out to take Dario's hand. "So lovely. My ivory angel! Come."

He had been staring at the prince's cock. It reared upward from his full ball-sack to slap against his firm abdomen. Solid like his body, but not so thick as it was incredibly long, it bobbed in rigid glory, as dark as his eyes and engorged with blood.

He pulled his gaze away and followed Adolfo to the winding staircase as they padded their way barefoot up the marble steps toward the prince's bedroom and the pleasures that loomed ahead.

The prince led Dario to the open balcony and leaned him up against the balustrade overlooking a moonlit garden. Beyond, the curve of the Bay of Naples shimmered in that same moonlight. To their right, Mount Vesuvius loomed, a dark mass against the starry heavens.

Bent over the railing, naked thighs spread wide, he groaned with disbelief as Adolfo knelt behind him and buried his bearded face in Dario's ass. The dark prince kissed Dario's asshole much as he had kissed his mouth earlier.

It was divine. The callused palms held the round cheeks of his ass apart as that handsome face rooted between. Tongue and lips attacked his quivering hole. They sucked him inside out. The tongue swabbed the quivering ass-lips then stabbed between.

The hands on his buttocks turned him as that wet mouth pulled out of his ass. He knew exactly what to do, squatting there with his naked back against the balcony as he engulfed the bobbing length of Adolfo's fuck-sword to the very root. He took it all, opening his gullet as he had opened his ass. With bare feet wide apart, his asshole yawned between his squatting buttocks, wet and quivering as his mouth slurped noisily over the magnificent length of the prince's dark prick.

He was lifted and turned again to lean out over the balcony. For a moment he was abandoned, then the heat of Adolfo's body pressed against his, that mighty cock throbbing as it settled between Dario's eager asscheeks.

"I have lubricated my prick—with olive oil," he whispered in Dario's ear, followed by a chuckle and a kiss to the lobe.

The tapered head slid into place as Dario held his breath in delicious anticipation. There was no pain, only a pulsing stretch as his prick entered him. Slowly and steadily, the hot meat speared him. He felt the twin orbs of the prince's balls settle against his quaking ass-crack.

Arms surrounded him. That prick fucked him, gently at first, then more quickly, then finally as savagely as he had dreamed of.

Lips kissed his neck, his cheek, his pale shoulder, as that steely cock impaled him while he whimpered and begged for more.

Then, all at once, the thrusting slap of hips against ass slowed. Adolfo began to whisper in his ear as that lengthy fuck-sword rode in and out with a measured, deep penetration.

"You were correct if you assumed I was looking for financial assistance when I invited you to dinner. But that is not all I would ask of you.

"I have been looking for someone to share my life with. I cannot do it alone. I do not want to do it alone. I fear I will die of a broken heart if I cannot escape the chains of my family and my background. I am sadly not cut out for the cutthroat politics of my family and the Italian aristocracy's hypocritical morality. I have been desperate to find a means of escape, and so all the carousing. Drunkenness seemed to help, but only to a point. I cannot go on as I have. Will you help me?"

Dario emitted a half-sob, half-groan. His dark prince had bared his soul. It was time to return the gift. "I will help you. I too have been desperate. Obsessed with money, and never satisfied with how much I have. I will love you if you choose to let me."

Out of the corner of his eye, he noticed the eruption. Mount Vesuvius!

They both stared in awe as a shower of molten sparks erupted skyward then rained down on the nearby slopes with brilliant orange-red glory. It was more a show than a dangerous threat, but nonetheless dramatic.

With the moonlight bathing them and that eruption punctuating their passionate promises, they fucked themselves to an ecstatic orgasm.

* * *

They did it together, which was a good sign that their love affair would stand the test of time. Dario sold off the expensive furnishings in the Da Conti villa while Adolfo used his connections to secure them residence at a Franciscan monastery out of Italy on the nearby Dalmatian coast.

There, they would rent an olive grove where Adolfo would revel in the daily life of an orchardist, and Dario would split his time between addressing the financial affairs of the monastery and painting, a dream he had abandoned for the lure of riches earned from banking.

Dario had his life's savings to help them get by, while Adolfo surprised his lover with a lavish gift that would do much to secure them a happy future. When the prince had allowed Dario to sell all his goods, he had not mentioned his personal jewels: a chest full of glittering gold and silver broaches and necklaces, studded with rubies, emeralds, and diamonds, worth a small fortune.

Two sides of a coin, different in so many ways, but keen to share all that they were, the pair disembarked on the shores of the Dalmatian island that was to be their home. Their former lives abandoned, their new life had begun.

CREOSOTE FLATS AND THE BIG SPREAD

Michael Bracken

West Texas creosote flats are covered with little more than creosote bush, yucca, and cholla cactus, and they stretch for miles in every direction. I know this because I traveled through the middle of a creosote flat for several hours after following my GPS system's instructions to turn off the main road and take a more direct route to my destination just across the New Mexico border.

The paved road gave way to gravel. Gravel gave way to dirt. Soon there wasn't much of a road at all. That's when my GPS system stopped working, my radiator blew fluid all over the engine, and I found myself standing alongside my overheated hybrid unable to get a signal on my iPhone.

Dressed for comfort, I wore penny loafers without socks, olive green cargo shorts, and a khaki polo shirt. I'd spent the previous day at the salon, where I'd had my hair styled and my eyebrows sugared. I looked fabulous, but fabulous wouldn't last long without air conditioning. I hadn't brought a change of clothes, and I hadn't thought to pack a hat.

I stared back in the direction I had come, knowing the main road was far behind me, and stared up the road in the direction I had been going, seeing the hard-packed dirt degrade into two parallel ruts. None of my three choices—go back, go forward, or remain where I was—appealed to me, and triple-digit heat did not enhance my decision-making ability.

After finishing the diet Dr Pepper I'd been nursing since lunch, I fashioned a head covering out of some napkins and a box from the chicken takeout place where I had stopped, doing my best to imitate the headgear worn by Foreign Legionnaires in all the old movies I'd watched with my father on Saturday afternoons. Then I began walking back the way I had come, hoping that a known destination was better than the unknown and that I would soon reach a point where my iPhone would pick up a signal.

Less than an hour later, I had blisters on both heels, the napkins covering my ears had begun to shred, and the musky citrus scent of the expensive aftershave I'd dabbed on that morning had been replaced by the overpowering stench of chicken grease. I stopped and tried my iPhone but still couldn't get a signal. I cursed my GPS system, my iPhone, and myself for being so reliant on technology that I hadn't prepared for the Texas that exists beyond the Austin city limits.

I had just started walking again when I heard a vaguely familiar sound behind me, a clip-clop I associated with old John Wayne movies. I spun around and found myself staring up into the deeply tanned face of a mouth-wateringly handsome cowboy astride a white mare. He must have been ten years my senior, wore a white Stetson with a low crown and wide brim over finger-length salt-and-pepper hair, a red bandanna tied loosely around his neck, a long-sleeved white shirt under a tan wool vest, faded Wrangler jeans under leather chaps, and well-worn Justin boots with silver spurs. Clearly I amused him—standing there in my dusty city clothes, wearing a chicken box for a hat—because the cowboy's pale blue eyes sparkled and the corners of his lips were pulled up in a grin I felt certain he was trying his best to suppress. He touched his index finger to the brim of his Stetson. "Afternoon."

"Afternoon," I replied.

"Where you headed?" he asked.

"Back where I came from."

"Where's that?'

"Austin."

"Long walk, ain't it?"

I held up my iPhone. "I was just planning to walk until I could get a signal on this."

He jerked a thumb over his shoulder. "That your car back there?"

I told him it was. I returned my iPhone to one pocket of my cargo shorts and resealed the Velcro flap.

"Where were you headed?"

"New Mexico."

"And why did you come this way?"

I told him about following the instructions of my GPS system, and his suppressed grin turned into a full-throated laugh.

"Lucky I found you," he said, "before the coyotes and the buzzards picked your carcass clean."

I shuddered.

The cowboy held out his hand. "Get on up here and I'll carry you back to the house."

As I reached out, he grasped my wrist, so I grasped his. Then he jerked me into the air like I weighed nothing at all and dropped me into the saddle behind him. The last horse I'd ridden was plugged into the front of a Safeway grocery store and cost my mother a quarter. Because I had no idea what I should do, I wrapped my arms around the cowboy's broad chest. He removed my hands from his chest and placed them on the saddle horn. Then I held on tight as he guided the mare off the road and through the creosote bush, yucca, and cholla cactus.

"What's your name?" I asked.

"Carl Rogers," he said over his shoulder. "My friends call me Buck."

It was my turn to suppress a grin.

"You?"

"Stephen Chambers," I told him. "My friends don't call often enough."

As we rode uphill, I quickly learned to appreciate Buck's leather chaps, and I tucked my bare legs as close behind his legs as I could to protect them from the cactus and other flora intent on filleting my shins. The mare's gentle gait and Buck's up-and-down movement caused his tight ass to rub against my crotch, causing a physical reaction I did not, at that time, appreciate. If Buck noticed my saddle horn jabbing into his backside, he was polite enough not to mention it.

When we crested the hill, I looked down at a compound that included a massive adobe-and-stone ranch house with a satellite dish beside it, a multicar garage with a small, single-prop airplane parked behind it, a barn with a corral containing two horses, and a pair of smaller buildings—one covered with solar panels—I didn't recognize. In the far distance I saw oil wells and longhorn cattle.

"Your place?" I asked.

"One of them."

I considered Buck's response as the mare made its way downhill and into the barn where we dismounted. Buck removed the horse's saddle and other tack, brushed it quickly, and then led it into the corral with the other horses. The mare promptly stuck its face in the water trough.

Buck clapped a big hand on my shoulder. "You look a mite parched," he said. "Let's head up to the house and see if we can quench your thirst."

He led me across the compound, through the back door, and into a kitchen that was a chef's stainless steel wet dream bigger than my entire Austin apartment. As I walked toward the sink, one of Buck's big paws lifted the chicken box from my head and dropped it into a waste can. Then he removed his Stetson and placed it on the counter before opening the refrigerator and offering me a selection of bottled beverages.

After I chose Shiner Bock, my host pulled out two bottles, opened one, and handed it to me. He opened the other bottle, downed most of it in one long swallow, and finished it before I had taken more than a couple of sips from mine. He tossed the empty on top of my chicken box hat and pulled another bottle from the fridge. Then he offered to show me the place.

Buck had furnished the ranch house in Texas chic—white limestone accent walls, oversized furniture with a Spanish influence, plenty of leather and cowhide, Texas Star drawer pulls—and many of the rooms appeared as if they had been set-designed as King Ranch catalog pages and were awaiting arrival of the photographer. The den, a room where Buck obviously spent much of his time, sported a wall-mounted big-screen television at one end, and overflowing floor-to-ceiling bookshelves covered the other three walls. A well-worn leather couch in the center of the room faced the television, and a paperback mystery, its spine broken, lay open and face down on one cushion. A colorful Mexican serape blanket lay in a wad on the other cushion, as if whoever had been using it had tossed it aside before rising.

The only other rooms that appeared lived in were the master bedroom and master bathroom upstairs. The unmade king-sized hacienda bed with headboard and footboard wrapped in nutmeg-colored leather dominated Buck's bedroom, and French doors on the east side of the room opposite the bed opened onto a broad porch. A stack of magazines littered one nightstand, a pile of laundry—apparently clean and waiting to be folded and put away—covered a leather sleeper chair.

When I followed Buck down the back stairs and into his office, the phone on the corner of his massive oak desk reminded me that I still hadn't contacted anyone about my disabled vehicle. I dug my iPhone from my pocket, checked it, and realized I still had no signal. I looked up at my host. "I need to contact someone about my car."

Buck picked up his desk phone and was soon giving the GPS coordinates of my abandoned hybrid to someone on the other end of the conversation.

After the conversation ended and Buck replaced the handset in its cradle, I asked, "You have a landline all the way out here?"

"Satellite phone," he explained. "Costs a pretty penny, but worth every cent."

"And my car?"

"My mechanic will pick it up in the morning and let us know what it needs as soon as he can work it in."

"What'll I do until then?"

He hesitated and I waited though the silence.

"Spend the night," he suggested. "Or, if you want, I can take you to town, drop you off at the roach motel."

Was the handsome cowboy hitting on me?

"A man gets lonely out here by himself," Buck said as we returned to the kitchen to replace our empty Shiner Bocks. His gaze slid over me in a way that could easily be misunderstood. "You can only read so many books and watch so many movies before you start craving a little human contact."

He *was* hitting on me. I looked up into his sparkling blue eyes and felt certain I could get lost in there.

Before I could respond, Buck continued. "You smell like fried chicken and it's making me hungry," he said. "Why don't you go upstairs and take a shower? While you do that I'll throw something on the grill for dinner."

He told me where to find towels and washcloths, and a few minutes later I was in the master bathroom stripping off my sweat-stained and chicken-scented clothing. The shower was as big as my entire bathroom, lined on the floor and three sides with glazed Mexican tile. A clear glass wall with a door in the middle constituted the fourth side.

After showering, I used antiseptic from the medicine cabinet for the scratches on my legs, splashed on some cologne from a bottle on the counter, and poked through the pile of clean laundry on the sleeper chair until I discovered gray drawstring sweatpants and a white T-shirt. Both were too big for me, but I made do.

I found Buck on the back patio, standing over a propane grill covered with foil-wrapped ears of corn and T-bones thick as decks of playing cards. When he saw me, he flipped the steaks onto plates, stacked the corn on a third plate, and carried everything to a picnic table where silverware, steak sauce, sticks of butter, and cold bottles of Shiner Bock waited.

"Good thing you're not one of those vegans," he said. "This is the best I could do on short notice."

"Don't worry," I told him as I stared into his eyes, "I enjoy a big piece of meat."

The grin I'd first seen when Buck found me earlier that day returned. He said, "I think we'll get along just fine."

I jabbed a knife into my steak, finding it charred on the outside and barely warm in the middle. Then I unwrapped an ear of corn, slathered it with butter, and began eating.

"So what were you aiming to do in New Mexico when you got there?" Buck asked.

"Housewarming. A former roommate and his current squeeze bought a place together."

"Shouldn't you call and let them know you won't be there?"

"I don't think they'll miss me," I said, but I didn't tell Buck why. I hadn't been invited to the housewarming and had awoken that morning intent on crashing the party and making a scene in some lame attempt to convince my former roommate that he was making a mistake. That's why I hadn't bothered to pack, was relying on my GPS system to get me to a place I'd never before been, and wasn't prepared when my hybrid overheated in the middle of a creosote flat. Which reminded me: "How did you find me?"

"Wasn't hard," Buck said around a mouthful of steak. "You'd been kicking up a rooster tail for hours. When the dust settled I knew something had to be wrong so I went for a look-see and there you were."

We talked about other things, including my job managing a used bookstore and lack of romantic prospects, and Buck told me about his inability to find his soul mate.

"I can buy companionship," he said, "but I can't buy love. That's why I spend most of my time here instead of the house in Aspen. In Aspen everybody's after my money. The only people likely to come out here would have to be interested in me."

"You believe in destiny?" I asked.

"How's that?"

"Maybe there was a reason my GPS system put me on the road to nowhere," I said, "because that road led me here, to you."

Buck smiled and lifted his bottle of Shiner Bock in toast. When I clinked my bottle against his, he said, "To destiny."

After dinner, I helped my host clean up. Then Buck went to the barn to tend to the horses while I nosed around his den. I found several first edition mystery novels, many of the literary classics I'd been forced to read in high school and college, and a variety of business books. From the plethora of cracked spines, I knew the books weren't just for display. I appreciated that. Other than the bookstore customers—none of whom were in my social circle—I didn't know anyone who read as much as I did.

I was thumbing through the paperback Buck had left face-down on the leather couch—a collection of mystery short stories—when he returned from the barn.

"I must smell a bit horsy," Buck said. "I'm headed upstairs for a shower."

After waiting several minutes, I followed my host. I slipped into the master bathroom, leaned back against the sink, and watched Buck through the glass wall of the shower. He was washing his salt-and-pepper hair, his eyes closed to keep out the shampoo, and I had time to really take him in. He had a cowboy tan; his face and arms were darkened and weathered, but the rest of his well-muscled body had not been exposed to the sun in several years.

Shampoo ran down Buck's powerful chest, and my gaze followed it over his six-pack abs, through the dark thatch of his pubic hair, and down the length of his thick phallus. I won't say he was hung like a horse, but I'm certain more than a few ponies would be jealous of what I saw dangling between Buck's thighs. I know it took my breath away.

Buck must have heard my intake of breath because he opened his eyes and looked at me through the glass. "I didn't hear you come in."

"I hope you don't mind."

"I don't have anything to hide." He squirted liquid soap on a washcloth and scrubbed his face, working his way down his torso to his legs. He straightened and returned his attention to the junction of his thighs and lathered up his pubic hair, causing his heavy ball sac to bounce up and down. Then he pulled back his foreskin and washed the head of his cock before washing the length of his stiffening shaft.

My own cock reacted to the sight and soon tented the front of the oversized sweatpants I'd pulled on after my shower earlier. I wet my lips with the tip of my tongue.

Buck cut off the water, reached out for a towel, and began drying himself. When he finished, he slung the towel around his shoulders and stepped from the shower stall.

I couldn't resist. I dropped to my knees on the bathroom floor, my face only inches from his fat phallus. When Buck didn't stop me, I wrapped my fist around his cock, pulled back his foreskin, and took the mushroom cap of his cock into my mouth. I painted his cock head with my tongue, tasting floral-scented soap as his cock stiffened, and then I slowly took his entire length into my mouth until his damp pubic hair tickled my nose, almost gagging because his cock was bigger than any I'd ever had before. I drew back and did it again.

As I cupped his heavy ball-sack in my palm, I kneaded his nuts. With the tip of one finger I stroked the sensitive spot behind his scrotum, and before long Buck couldn't restrain himself. He wrapped his thick fingers around the back of my head and face-fucked me, driving his thick cock in and out of my mouth, his balls bouncing against my chin. I grabbed his muscular thighs and felt him tense just before he came, so I was ready for the flood of warm cum he fired against the back of my throat, and I swallowed again and again and held his slowly deflating cock in my mouth until I had licked away the last drop of cum.

When I finally released my oral grip on Buck's cock, he lifted me to my feet.

"That's a good start," he said as he peeled his T-shirt off of me and untied the drawstring of the sweatpants I was wearing. They dropped to the floor and pooled around my ankles, revealing my own still-erect cock.

I stepped out of the sweatpants and turned. I'd seen lube in Buck's medicine cabinet when I'd been rooting around for the antiseptic, and I knew we'd need it. I pulled open the cabinet and wrapped my fingers around the tube of lube just as Buck spun me back around to face him.

He lifted me onto the countertop, spread my legs, and stepped between them. His cock was already half-erect and was rising rapidly as he slid a condom over it. I opened the lube, squirted a glob on my fingers, and slathered it over his swollen cock head. He grabbed my legs behind the knees and lifted until he had my body at the angle he wanted. Then he pressed his lube-covered cock against the tight pucker of my ass and drove forward, causing me to gasp as he buried himself inside me.

I was surprised and excited at the same time. No lover had ever taken me like this and I had never before been able to stare into my lover's eyes as we fucked. Buck pulled back and pushed forward, his slick shaft rubbing against the underside of my ball-sack as he drove into me, exciting me. I reached between us, wrapped my fist around my own turgid cock, and began pumping.

Buck stared into my eyes, never once looking away, his pale blue eyes mesmerizing me. I came first, firing warm spunk all over my abdomen. That seemed to excite Buck because he began pumping harder, faster.

Then, with one final, powerful thrust that made my ass squeak against the countertop as he pushed me backward, Buck came.

Neither of us moved as the cowboy's cock throbbed within me and we stared deep into one another's eyes until his cock finally softened enough for him to easily pull free.

I'd been ridden hard; would I be put away wet?

Not by this cowboy.

We cleaned up, and then Buck led me to the hacienda bed, where I finally told him exactly why I'd been on my way to a housewarming in New Mexico.

"You still in love with your ex-roommate?"

"No," I admitted. "I think I just wanted to cause him as much pain as he'd caused me when he moved out."

"And now?"

"Now I realize what a stupid idea that was."

"But it brought you here, to my bed," Buck said.

I smiled, snuggled against him, and fell asleep with Buck's arms wrapped around me.

The sun blasted through the eastern-facing French doors the next morning, waking me. Buck had one arm over his eyes, and the bright light didn't seem to bother him. I slipped out of bed, opened the French doors, and stood naked on the balcony. I couldn't see any of the longhorn cattle from where I stood, but I could make out a couple of the oil wells in the far, far distance of my host's big spread.

I glanced back into the bedroom. Buck had kicked off the sheet and his thick phallus lay flaccid against his thigh, reminding me of the hard ride he'd given me the previous evening.

Buck's mechanic would be retrieving my dead hybrid later that morning and could take all the time in the world repairing it, because I was in no hurry to leave. I crawled back into bed with Buck, took the head of his cock in my mouth, and slowly woke my handsome cowboy.

ABOUT THE AUTHORS

JANINE ASHBLESS is the author of five books of paranormal and fantasy erotica published by Black Lace and has had short stories published in numerous anthologies including *Fairy Tale Lust* (Cleis, 2010). She blogs about minotaurs, Victorian art, and writing dirty at www.janineashbless.blogspot.com.

MICHAEL BRACKEN's short fiction has been published in *Best Gay Romance 2010, Biker Boys, Country Boys, Freshmen, Homo Thugs, Hot Blood: Strange Bedfellows, The Mammoth Book of Erotic Confessions, The Mammoth Book of Best New Erotica 4, Muscle Men, Teammates, Ultimate Gay Erotica 2006,* and many other anthologies and periodicals.

HEIDI CHAMPA found her handsome prince many years ago, but a good story about knights on white horses gets her every time. Her work has been published in numerous anthologies such as *College Boys, Like Magnets We Attract, Skater Boys,* and *Hard Working Men.* Find more at heidichampa.blogspot.com.

BONNIE DEE began telling stories as a child. Whenever there was a sleepover, she was the designated ghost tale teller, guaranteed to frighten and thrill with macabre tales. You can find more of her work at bonniedee.com.

S. A. GARCIA can never decide between red or white. Nor can S.A. decide between creating visual art or word art so succumbing to both urges feels logical. S.A. spins the talents in between cooking, drinking, sitting before the computer far more than is healthy, and growing legal herbs and oddly named flowers.

Depending on publication dates, this may be **FOX LEE**'s first published story. Then again, "Getting Visual," scheduled to appear in the erotic anthology, *Rock and Roll Over* (STARbooks Press) may have that honor instead.

J. L. MERROW read natural sciences at Cambridge, where she learned many things, chief among them was that she never wanted to see the inside of a lab ever again. Her one regret is that she never mastered the ability of punting one-handed whilst holding a glass of champagne. Her latest novella, *Pricks and Pragmatism*, is available from Samhain Publishing. Find her online at www.jlmerrow.com.

AARON MICHAELS's fiction has appeared in numerous anthologies, including *Skater Boys, Surfer Boys*, and *Hard Hats*, as well as at online at TorquereBooks.com. Aaron lives in northern Nevada and can be found on the web at www.aaron-michaels.com.

RED MORGAN lives in Yorkshire, England. Red is working on a second novel, a murder mystery based in Los Angeles and Yorkshire.

English through and through, **JOSEPHINE MYLES** is addicted to tea and already well on the way to becoming a disreputable eccentric. She has recently had gay erotic stories published in the anthologies *Like That Spark, Necking* and *Mine*. Visit her blog at josephine-myles.livejournal.com.

GREGORY L. NORRIS is a full-time writer who appears regularly in national magazines and fiction anthologies. A former writer at *Sci Fi,* he worked as a screenwriter on Paramount TV's *Star Trek: Voyager* and is the author of the handbook to all-things-Sunnydale, *The Q Guide to Buffy the Vampire Slayer*. He writes and lives in the outer limits of New Hampshire.

ROB ROSEN is author of *Sparkle: The Queerest Book You'll Ever Love* and *Divas Las Vegas* (Cleis Press), winner of the 2010 TLA Gaybies for Best Gay Fiction. His work has appeared in more than a hundred anthologies, notably *Best Gay Love Stories 2006, Best Gay Romance (2007, 2008, 2009,* and *2010), Best Gay Love Stories: New York City, Best Gay Love Stories: Summer Flings, Ultimate Gay Erotica 2008* and *2009,* and *Best Gay Love Stories 2009*. Visit him at www.therobrosen.com.

Residing on English Bay in Vancouver, Canada, **JAY STARRE** pumps out erotic fiction for gay men's magazines and gay fiction anthologies. These include B*est Gay Romance 2008, Best Gay Bondage, Bears, Surfer Boys,* and *Special Forces,* all from Cleis Press. He is the author of two historical erotic novels, *The Erotic Tales of the Knights Templars* and *The Lusty Adventures of the Knossos Prince*.

ABOUT
THE EDITOR

NEIL PLAKCY is the editor of *Hard Hats, Surfer Boys,* and *Skater Boys,* all gay erotic anthologies from Cleis Press. He is the author of the *Mahu* series about openly gay Honolulu homicide detective Kimo Kanapa'aka and the *Have Body, Will Guard* series about bodyguards Aidan Greene and Liam McCullough. The author of *Paws and Reflect,* he also writes the book column for GayWired.com. He lives in South Florida. Visit Neil at www.mahubooks.com.